THE FOURTH HORSEMAN

It was almost midnight on Friday the thirteenth when the man in black entered the hotel where Willard Dull, Government Agent, was sitting reading a book. As the stranger retired to his room, Dull took a look at the register. The man had signed himself as 'Death' from 'Hell'. Before midnight chimed, two men were dead, both killed by the man in black. Dull suddenly realised that all his plans to trap a gang of payroll robbers were about to fall apart—unless he could stop Death from reaping a grim harvest.

THE FOURTH HORSEMAN

by
Jack Giles

Dales Large Print Books
Long Preston, North Yorkshire,
England.

British Library Cataloguing in Publication Data.

Giles, Jack
    The fourth horseman.

    A catalogue record for this book is
    available from the British Library

    ISBN 1-85389-897-X pbk

First published in Great Britain by Robert Hale Ltd., 1994

Copyright © 1994 by Jack Giles

Cover illustration © Chicharro by arrangement with Allied
Artists

Published in Large Print 1999 by arrangement with Robert
Hale Ltd.

Dales Large Print is an imprint of
Library Magna Books Ltd.
Printed and bound in Great Britain by
T.J. International Ltd., Cornwall, PL28 8RW.

ONE

It was Friday 13th.

All day it had been hot and oppressive. The kind of day that made men sweat, lazy and lethargic. Even at sunset there had been no respite for the heat of the day seemed to be locked up in the buildings that made up the town of Oakridge.

Heat still lingered out on the street, a warm residue that made stragglers search for some kind of cool shade.

The saloons at the far end of town did a roaring trade with both cattlemen and townsfolk alike. Though the seekers of relief did not find it in the consumption of lukewarm beer. It just slaked thirsts, replaced lost fluids and made the drinker order more of the same, while the saloon owners counted the profit.

One man did not boast a profit, though, and that was Jason Bates who owned the Oakridge Hotel. Time and again he had told his mother that they should operate a small bar, but she would not have it.

Who needed Friday 13th? he thought. Every day was bad for him, ever since his father had died and his mother had chosen to come and live with him. She had taken command of his hotel and his life—which had cost him a loving and caring wife.

He glanced at the clock. Ten o'clock. Another half an hour and the night clerk would turn up and then he could go to bed.

Jason Bates glanced over at the *chaise-longue* just by the open double doors where a resident sat, sprawled out; to all intents and purposes reading a thick leather-bound book, yet throwing covert glances out of the big picture window towards the saloon opposite.

If the man was not sitting in one of the rockers outside, then that *chaise* seemed to be for his sole use. Nothing had changed: the same old routine had been followed for the last ten days.

Bates had his suspicions, for it did not take long for a rumour to come down from Summerhill forty miles away, that the lawman there had been gunned down and that this particular hotel guest had disappeared soon after. Not that he had done the killing, everyone knew who had, but there was an opinion that this book-reader had some connection.

Bates sighed heavily, glanced again at the clock, his gaze dropping to stare at the heavy brass pendulum swinging from side to side, scything away the remnants of the day.

He glowered at the book-reader. 'You got enough light, Mr Dull?'

Willard Dull glanced up. 'Enough thanks.' He noticed the time. 'Figure you're hinting at something. You want to turn in early,

I'll keep an eye on things till the help arrives.'

Bates mumbled something unintelligible that was not very complimentary. All he was doing was to try and break the monotony. If Dull had heard anything, he showed no sign as he returned his attention back to the book, just as a page flicked up.

A whisper of cool breeze swept through the open doors. A prelude to the gusts that came in increasing waves down the street from the cast.

'A storm coming,' Dull stated, informatively, proving that humanity was not the only nature that he studied.

A lightning flash lit up the dimly lit hotel foyer, revealing Bates's startled expression which faded to one of shock as he ducked at the first explosive crack of thunder.

Bates grinned, weakly. 'Never can stand thunder. Not since the war.'

'War can do that to a man,' Dull conceded, without a trace of sympathy.

'You get involved?' Bates asked.

'Some,' Dull shrugged, trying to return to his book.

'I was in from the start,' Bates mentioned. 'Got through unscathed—except for this fear of thunder. You?'

Dull put his book aside, slightly miffed that the hotel owner had not taken the hint.

'No one goes into a war and comes out unscathed,' Dull stated, bluntly. 'On some you see the scars; others—well, they're like you and me. No one ever sees them. No one knows about them until you reveal them. Just as you have done by telling me about your fear.'

Bates was not listening. He was staring at the doorway. Not at the sudden deluge of lightning-lit rain that had turned the hard-packed dirt road to a muddy river, but at the giant of a man who had appeared in the doorway.

He was tall. Over six feet six inches and weighing about three hundred pounds—all of it solid muscle. Most of his face was hidden by the wide brim of a black, low, round-crowned hat. His round chin was well bristled and his black hair hung shoulder length, like wet rats' tails over the collar of his knee-length black overcoat. His whole attire was black. Shirt, vest, pants, boots and gunbelt and leather gloves. Just the one hue.

Right then, Bates would have bet money that if he could see the stranger's face his skin would be black also. In that he was wrong. The skin was pale, only the narrowed eyes were dark—almost black.

Dull, his attention now focused on this new arrival, watched the man approach an open-mouthed Bates.

'Ye-yes, sir,' Bates gulped.

'A room,' the stranger stated, his tone cold; like iced gravel.

'Only one room available,' Bates mentioned nervously, half-turning to point at the key board from which one key hung on its hook. 'Room thirteen.' He let loose a false laugh. 'Most folks shy away from that one.'

'A room's a room,' the stranger stated, indifferently.

'Guess you're right at that,' Bates offered, lightly.

'I'm not superstitious,' the stranger said, as he reached for the register and inkstand.

'I suppose thirteen has to be lucky for some,' Dull said, wanting to be a part of the small-talk. Besides he wanted to draw the man's attention for he wanted to see his face.

The stranger obliged. He turned and lifted his head just enough for Dull to make out the features. Dull blinked as a question rose to his lips that died as the stranger spoke.

'Unlucky for most.'

There seemed to be a hidden meaning behind those words. Dull shuddered, as though a sixth sense was warning him against something. He sought solace in the words of his book but concentration eluded him as that expressionless, pale face burned into his mind.

Dull waited until the stranger had climbed the stairs and heard the soft click of a door shutting before he put the book to one side and approached the desk.

'This has to be a joke,' Bates gulped, turning the register around so that Dull could see the latest entry.

The entry showed under the respective headings of *Name, Town and Occupation— Death; Hell; You don't want to know.*

'All very melodramatic,' Dull grunted; then with a sense of foreboding, 'But no joke.' He shuddered. 'I figure he has an appointment here.'

TWO

Dull returned to the *chaise-longue* and picked up his book, but the words no longer commanded his interest. Like a ghost, that pale face kept drifting through his mind. Familiar yet unfamiliar. He had studied the man and categorized him as a killer.

Like a drowning man, Dull began to search his memory looking for an encounter where their paths might have crossed. Nowhere could he recall seeing this one man.

Summerhill.

But that man had not been there. Yet that sixth sense linked the two. Dull sat there lost in thought, retracing all that had happened in that town, unaware that the pale-faced stranger was doing the same.

Time had passed by leaving Calvin Nicholls older and perhaps a little wiser. When he had come to Summerhill, it had been just a one street stopover that marked a point on the road from some place to elsewhere. Then the railroad came and changed everything. Suddenly, there were overflowing stockyards, abattoirs, tanneries, warehouses: an industrial growth that left the average person spinning.

Progress made him feel older than his thirty-two years of age. He longed for the old, slower days in an age that demanded change. Maybe, it was time to go home and see his father and brother; he would shrug that thought away. What had happened to Summerhill had probably happened there too. Progress was eating into everything. Forty miles to the east, a new town had risen up alongside the railroad. A place called Oakridge that was twice the size of the town he tried to police.

Not that there was much he could

do in that direction either. He had two deputies and the town council were too tight-fisted to pay the wages for more. The increase in the population required more men to enforce the law against the rowdier elements. No one listened, not even when the longest serving deputy, Sam Vennor, was shot down in cold blood. By sheer fortune Calvin Nicholls and his remaining deputy managed to arrest the gunmen and lock them up in the new brick-built jailhouse.

The town council had the money for that and the new brick-built courthouse, but not for men—not for wages: only for prestige. The only satisfaction that Calvin Nicholls could glean from the situation was that come the following year not many of the council would still be in office.

That was the future. Calvin was more concerned with the present. Two problems. One was getting eight men to the courthouse to face the circuit judge. The other was Sam Vennor's son, Jason.

A young hot-head who wanted frontier justice rather than the due process of law; neither did he have any faith in the town marshal's ability as a prosecutor. Against all that Jason Vennor was just the kind of person whom Calvin could enlist as a deputy; but who would have to occupy one of the cells for his own safety until the trial was over.

He walked the street searching for likely trouble spots before concluding that every inch of the route would be a problem. He paused at the steps of the courthouse and looked up at the blindfolded statue of justice that stood above the canopied entrance. It was too opulent, just like the black and white marble floors and the marble columns inside.

The only thing in its favour was that the interior was cool. The silence echoed in his ears. A haven with a kind of serenity after the bustle outside.

A long hall stretched out in front of him. To the left, a row of offices and interview rooms; to the right, a courtroom. A marble and wrought-iron staircase rose to a second floor with a similar layout; an example of forward planning by a town council who expected the town to become the legal centre for the county. They were even advertising for two judges to take up permanent posts, rather than rely on a circuit judge who had to hear cases from trespass to murder in the shortest possible time during the course of one week in every eight.

It was strange how the council managed to veer between long-sightedness and short, Calvin thought, as he entered the courtroom to survey the arena for his opening legal battle. He strode down the aisle between the spectators' pews to the large tables that faced the rostrum where the judge would sit. Again he shook his head as he took in the oak panelling, and the green leatherwork on the desks and chairs. No expense spared.

Except when it came to hiring a public

prosecutor. Someone with legal training who could fence with an eloquent defence lawyer. Why did they need one, when they had an able town marshal who was capable of doing that job? Most important of all they did not have to pay two jobs, when they were already paying Calvin Nicholls.

He closed his eyes and shook his head. One more burden and he would quit. If the eight men accused of robbery and murder were acquitted because of his ineptitude as a lawyer, then he would throw away his badge. He would not be the scapegoat for the town council's pennypinching when it came to important matters. Prestige did nothing for law and order.

When he felt this low, he regretted his decision to turn down the offer of policing Dodge City. Instead, it was a friend of his, Ed Masterson, who took the job. He supposed that he could ask Ed for a job, but, he guessed, home would beckon first.

Home. Where, he wondered, was home?

He had been away for so long. Seven? Eight years? Calvin had lost track of time. Summerhill was more his home, than the two-bit town on the Arizona-Texas border, that he had grown up in. Where his mother was buried. Where ... He did not want to think about the reason he had left. Nor about the way his father had disowned him. His brother had tried to understand.

Calvin allowed himself a smile. Poor old Asa, always the butt of their pa's sick sense of humour; yet so understanding. He listened and tried to find answers to other people's problems. Not this one, though; there was nothing that Asa had been able to do to heal the rift between father and son. So Calvin had walked away and opened a grocery store in the, then, small town of Summerhill. Asa knew where he was, but had never been in contact. Then again, nor had Calvin taken the trouble to write home.

So he shoved the thoughts of home

aside and took one last look around the courtroom. This was where his own future stood in the balance. Perhaps, for once, judgement would fall in his favour.

As he turned his back on the judge's bench, he became aware of a low drone. He moved to the right, closer to the door that opened on to the judge's chambers. Two men were talking, their conversation becoming heated. Despite that Calvin could only catch the occasional word at first.

' ... twenty years.' The voice was cracked with age; Calvin recognized it as that of Judge John D. Cox. 'Took a bribe ...'

'Do as ...' came the second voice, sharp, deep and authoritative; also familiar, though Calvin could not place it. ' ... go free ... or you'll never ...'

The voices came and went as though both men were frightened of being overheard, while sure in their own minds that they were alone in the building. Calvin knew that something was being threatened, but became indecisive. Should he intervene or just walk away and do nothing until an official complaint was made.

' ... this once,' the judge gave in weakly. ' ... debts to pay ... never again ...'

Cal's blood ran cold. A deal had been made in his hearing, but he was not quite sure how it affected him. He found it difficult to believe that the straight and honest man he knew the judge to be, could accept a bribe. Yet, as he backed away from the door and slid beneath the judge's bench, he would have to see who was offering the bribe.

The door handle rattled, then turned and the door swung wide and a tall, distinguished-looking man with greying, red hair stepped out.

'Never again,' Cox roared emphatically, thumping his desk. 'You hear me, Tunbridge?'

Major Samuel Tunbridge, a town councillor and owner of one of the more prestigious hotels and two of the more dubious saloons and gaming-houses at the opposite end of town, stood rock still. Then, slowly, deliberately, about-turned to face the judge.

'You are bought for ever more, Cox,' the hawk-faced Tunbridge sneered. 'I own you. Everyone has their price or a weakness that can be exploited. That is why I can occupy a lowly place in society yet wield more power than the mayor and the whole damn town council put together.'

He watched the judge slump behind his desk. A broken man for whom Tunbridge felt nothing but contempt. He could not respect weak men and the strong were always a challenge; men, like the seemingly incorruptible town marshal—and if he had a weakness, Tunbridge had not found it.

Tunbridge closed the door and ambled over to the bench, to stare up at the miniature statue of justice that stood on a marble plinth above the chair. Blind justice, who could not see what was happening to her.

Then Calvin was there. Eyes locked with those of Tunbridge, who managed to mask his surprise at the lawman's presence.

'Why would you want to buy a judge?' Calvin asked.

'That is what I like about you, Calvin,' Tunbridge smiled, though his eyes did not echo any humour. 'Direct and to the point. Though it is none of your business I will explain something to you. I have a small business venture that should make me a considerable profit. If I profit—the town benefits. However, a certain legal complication has set in—the judge must make a ruling. In the interests of this town, I require the judge to make the right decision. The law is always indecisive or unclear; judge's give their ruling and everything becomes clear. A simple matter that makes precedents.'

Calvin did not believe one word of this explanation.

'So who goes free?' he asked.

Tunbridge nodded sagely, now that

he knew how much the lawman had overheard.

'The town,' Tunbridge replied, sternly, with a finality that meant he would answer no more questions. 'Now, I have other matters that need my attention. So I bid you—good day.'

He turned, abruptly, and strode up the aisle. Then paused as though he had just thought of something.

'Calvin, you heard nothing,' Tunbridge advised, then smiled. 'You would like some support in your application for more deputies.'

'I'm not that desperate,' Calvin stated, blandly.

Tunbridge nodded. 'No. I did not think you were.'

Calvin watched the doors close, then relaxed a little, for his mind was still wrestling with what he had overheard and what Tunbridge had explained to him. Something did not seem right. The words 'go free' kept coming back to him.

If it was someone, then it had to be eight someones. The men who had killed Sam Vennor. Except that there was nothing that he was aware of, then, that could interest Tunbridge.

'You heard everything?' Judge Cox asked, incredulously, almost shrinking deeper into the soft leather chair.

Calvin stood on the other side of the desk, his face a mask of contempt. Cox seemed to shrink even more and started to squirm.

'I know you've been bought,' Calvin persisted.

'It's out of my hands now.' Cox tried to bluff his way out of the hole he was in.

'No it's not,' Calvin countered. 'Corruption of court officials is an offence—'

'Now you stop right there,' Cox struggled, but he was going to fight back. 'What evidence do you have? Do you think that either Tunbridge or myself are going to admit that such a conversation took place?

No money has changed hands. You have nothing, young man; nothing at all. Now kindly leave my office.'

Calvin glared at the small, round-shouldered man; whose mane of grey hair had escaped from its usual style to fall about his thin-featured face.

'Maybe, you're right,' the lawman nodded. 'But you think on this: if you can't uphold your office, then you'd best think about stepping down.'

'How dare you? You are making a threat,' the judge blustered, finding a little more courage.

Calvin shook his head. 'A promise. You do as Tunbridge told you and I'll make it known you're not straight and honest.'

'And if my decision conforms to what Tunbridge wants,' the judge enquired, 'and I do not accept the bribe? What then?'

'Why not just adjourn the case?' Calvin offered. 'Let it go to another venue and another judge. Solves the problem.'

'Why not, indeed,' Cox smiled. 'Let me sleep on it.'

'Give it thought, Your Honour,' Calvin prompted.

With Cox's assurance that he would, the lawman left the office unaware that the judge was letting loose a sigh of relief.

The judge went to his washroom where he splashed cold water over his face. He glanced at the mirror to look at the reflection over his shoulder.

'You heard all that?' Cox asked, of the thick-set man who sat on the commode.

'Every word,' the man said, with a strong eastern accent. 'That lawman has me worried.'

Cox turned around as he towelled his face dry. 'There is no doubt that he knows what is going on.'

'Just suspicions,' the Easterner advised. 'Nothing to worry about just yet.'

The Easterner stood six feet tall with a heavy build and features. His eyes were light blue and deceptively gentle. His sandy-coloured hair was close cropped. The suit he wore was a charcoal grey with a thin pinstripe and a definite city cut. Despite the eastern style of clothes, he affected hand-tooled Western-style black boots and a roll-brimmed white stetson.

The Easterner strolled into the judge's office and took up a position by the window, so that he could look up and down the alley between the courthouse and the building alongside.

'Nervous, John?' he asked, politely.

'Wouldn't you be?' Cox fired back. 'How would you feel, if you were in my position?'

The Easterner chewed, thoughtfully, at the inside of his mouth for a few moments.

'Maybe,' he conceded, pushing himself away from the window and withdrawing further back into the room to a position where he could observe both the judge and view through the window, at the same time.

'I feel like a pig, caught in the middle,'

Cox confessed, leaning forward to steeple his fingers on which he balanced his chin and resting his elbows on the edge of the desk. 'First Tunbridge and now Nicholls.'

'Who knows nothing,' the other reminded him. 'The important thing is that MacGrath and his men go free tomorrow.'

'They will,' Cox confirmed with a resigned sigh. 'And when they do, Nicholls will put two and two together and my life as a judge will be over.'

'It is necessary, John,' he was reminded. 'I went through everything with you.'

Cox shook his head. 'That is not the point, Dull. I find the whole matter—distasteful. In all my years I have never had to accept a bribe.'

Willard Dull smiled, benevolently. 'Nor will you have to do it again. You will be taken care of. You can retire and live on a nice fat pension from the government for the rest of your life.'

'I do not see the difference,' Cox said, wearily. 'What is the difference between what Tunbridge offered and what you are promising? Either way my reputation is in ruins because I am accepting a bribe.'

Dull examined his fingers for a moment, then looked at the judge.

There was no gentleness in his eyes when he said, 'You were asked to co-operate with us. That is what you are doing. The government is simply paying you compensation for the damage to your reputation. Nothing more.'

'That is not the way I see it,' Cox retorted. 'And what about Nicholls? Surely, it would be in order to let him know what it is that is going on.'

'None of his business, John,' Dull stated, simply. 'However, if it helps to ease your conscience, I will tell him what he needs to know. And then, because I will need his help.'

'You do not know Nicholls,' Cox snorted. 'He is a fair man and does a good job, but you cross him—'

'He will do exactly as he is told to,' Dull assured the judge.

Nicholls would, Dull thought to himself, because he knew something that the lawman would not spread about town. Everyone had a weakness and Dull was an expert at exploiting them; he could give lessons to manipulators like Tunbridge.

'Do not be so sure,' Cox warned.

Warmth returned to Dull's eyes. 'We shall see. Well, my business with you is at an end. I think I will go and enjoy a good meal at Major Tunbridge's hotel, then enjoy a good book. See you in court tomorrow.'

With that Willard Dull left the judge alone to ponder on things that the smooth talking Easterner had said. Or not said.

Dull had told him the things that he needed to know, but not the whole story. Nor could he see what the connection was between Major Tunbridge and a bunch of killers and robbers led by a man called Abel MacGrath.

He decided that there was no point in speculating. Then he smiled to himself. It was time for lunch, so he thought that it might be a good idea to join Dull; whether to embarrass the Easterner or learn something by observation he was not quite sure.

As it turned out Major Tunbridge was not around, but Dull did not inform Cox during the small talk over dinner, that the object of their interest was locked in his office in conference, which was causing Dull some concern for he, for once, did not know what was going on.

Had Cox known this, he might have seen some humour in the situation.

THREE

It was the day of the trial.

Abel MacGrath sat on the edge of the bunk, his eyes narrow and thoughtful as he watched the middle-aged deputy finish off some paperwork and tuck it away in the desk drawer.

MacGrath stood up and stretched, then ran a hand over his grey, stubbled chin before ambling over to the barred window. The sky was a light shade of blue; cool blue. Yet the heat of the day was building to the extent that the cell was already hot and stuffy. Still, MacGrath thought, it was going to be a good day.

He glanced around at the double-tiered bunks and then at the floor where two men slept on straw mattresses under grey blankets, then through the bars to the cell opposite where another four men slept, similarly.

Eight men—nine if you included Bryden Royce who stood bodyguard down at the Golden Eagle gambling saloon. Nine men out of the fifty who rode out of Gettysburgh under Colonel Abraham Crandell eleven years ago. Crandell's Comanches. The Federal Army's answer to the likes of Quantrill and Moseby. Raiders who brought death, destruction and mayhem to those States which supported the South in the bitter Civil War. By the end of the war there were still twenty or so of them left alive, but Crandell was dead. He had been arrested after the surrender and hanged; the rest of the survivors were hunted down. It had been one thing to carry out orders in war, another thing come the peace. A man got punished for doing as he was told.

As time passed, so men died. Some rode away, hoping to live out the rest of their lives in anonymity. Good luck to them,

MacGrath thought.

Now there were just the nine of them: raiders in war and continuing the job in the peace.

The three red-haired Johnson brothers: they enjoyed what they did. Rustling, bank hold-ups, stage and train robberies they took in their stride because it meant money in their pockets and they could enjoy the high life for a while. Three brothers who were a unit within a unit, often going solo when their pockets started to empty.

Sharing their cell was a silent, dark-skinned man called Byrd. Nobody knew much about him except that he was dependable. Maybe he had no other place to go and by riding with MacGrath and the others he got a sense of belonging.

MacGrath looked at the floor where a mop of thinning grey hair stuck out from beneath a blanket. It belonged to Hepburn Lance, a short rotund man in his late fifties, who usually lived with a whore half his age down in Oakridge. He had been with the raiders from the beginning but he had a quirk—he enjoyed killing. A man like that couldn't retire, MacGrath supposed, not until someone did the job for him.

If MacGrath had a reliable lieutenant, then it had to be Deke Tinsley who at that point was swinging his legs over the edge of the top bunk and sitting up. They shared one thing in common—a sense of injustice. Men they had known had been hanged for serving the country they had fought for. The now United States of America owed them. At least that was how they viewed the situation.

Cole Colby could have been put in that same category but he was more concerned with another kind of injustice. They put their lives on the line so that one man could profit without any risk to himself. They only got half of everything that they took and of late he had made no bones about the way he felt. No one took much notice of the tall, gangly grouser.

'Today's the day,' Tinsley mentioned, sliding from the bunk, his bootheels thudding on to the paved floor within an inch of Lance's head.

Lance woke up with an ugly look in his eye and an expletive exploding from his lips.

'One day,' the old man promised.

'Possibly.' Tinsley grinned easily, looking across at the heavily lined face and the alert grey eyes of Abel MacGrath.

'Don't look at me,' MacGrath commented. 'You got an argument, you settle it.'

Tinsley held out his arms, hands palm upwards and adopting an expression of innocence. 'I've got no argument. Not my fault if this old man always wakes up crotchety.'

Hepburn Lance tried to roll out of bed, but the blankets snagged his ankles together.

'Not so much of the "old",' Lance roared. 'You ain't so young yerself.'

Abel MacGrath had to smile. Lance was right. None of them was that young anymore. He was forty-nine. Tinsley in his early forties. Mel Johnson in his mid-twenties was the youngest. Most of us, he mused, are getting too old for all this.

Suddenly, he felt frustrated. He had just acknowledged his age and realized that he achieved nothing that he could be proud of. Right then he would have given anything to walk out of that cell, mount a horse and ride away. Be free. More important, right then, to be his own man.

Tinsley could see the change that swept over MacGrath. Any other time and he would have taken Abel to one side and persuaded him to confide in him. Now was not the time and place.

Besides, Cole Colby was up and striding towards the iron-barred door, which he proceeded to rattle.

'Deputy,' he roared, 'where's my breakfast?'

MacGrath and Tinsley exchanged knowing glances. Nothing changed; the routine of the last few days was being followed. Colby was thinking of his stomach and made sure that everyone else knew it.

The middle-aged Jed Farley, the longest serving deputy, allowed Colby to batter the door for a good five minutes. Then levered himself, lazily, out of his chair and ambled over to the cell.

'Good morning, Cole,' Jed greeted, lightly, his youngish looking face wreathed in a smile. 'Usual problem?'

'I'm damned hungry,' Colby snarled.

'I would've thought you'd have got the hang of the routine by now,' Jed told him. 'Breakfast at nine.' Then as an afterthought, 'You know, Cole, you should think yourself lucky. You get it all nice and easy here. But you know when that judge sentences you, you will go to a State penitentiary and there—' He paused for effect and his voice was harsh when he continued. 'You serve hard time.

Make no mistake. So enjoy a little luxury while you can.'

Colby cursed, but Jed Farley chose to ignore him and walked away back to the desk, where he put his feet up and watched the world pass by the window.

He was feeling a little resentful that he was on duty this particular day. It should have been his day off. He wanted to be out on that rough patch of ground at the back of his small house playing baseball with his three young sons. It was a game he had picked up in the army and was determined to teach it to the boys.

Instead he had to sit around waiting for the other deputy, Cliff Phelan to turn up, so that he could spend an hour at home and have a proper breakfast, put his feet up and have a light nap.

As usual, the young drifter, who had taken the job a month before was demonstrating his main weakness—by never being where he was supposed to be, on time.

Jed had always been taught to be

punctual and could never understand a generation that believed in doing things when they were ready and not when they were supposed to be done.

At which point Phelan sauntered into the office with a casual, 'Hi.'

'Thank you for coming by,' Jed said with sarcasm. 'I'll have just enough time to eat my breakfast before I have to rush back here.'

'No sweat, Jed,' the youngster grinned. 'Just you go on and take your time. I ain't goin' no place.'

Jed was tempted to take a swipe at the cheeky kid, instead changed his mind and slammed the door on the way out.

Phelan ambled over to the cells.

'Hi fellas!' he grinned. 'Not long to go.'

Colby glared at him. 'You know, kid, one day you're going to get yours.'

'Maybe,' Phelan shrugged. 'An' if I do, the other fella's goin' to have to be good.'

'Don't argue with the boy, Cole.' A piece of good advice from Deke Tinsley. 'He's just trying to rile you up.' Then to Phelan, 'You know, boy, there's a time to talk and a time to know when to keep quiet.'

'Time to talk,' Phelan said, the bantering tone lost as his expression became serious. 'The word is you'll be free today. You're all to scatter but be sure you meet up in Oakridge three weeks from now. One thing you gotta do first,'—he allowed himself a smile,—'you gotta make a killing.'

Calvin Nicholls ate a hearty breakfast. Then he sat back to enjoy a second cup of coffee. He admitted to himself that the day he had decided to lodge with the widow Pam Ross, was the best decision he had ever made. She was about his age with a good figure and a kind, attentive manner, someone he could confide in and she in him. Their relationship was almost like husband and wife without the trimmings.

At night he could go to his own room in the guest-house and sleep peacefully in his own bed—which was not the way Pam wanted it, and he knew it, but he said nothing because he did not want to hurt her.

'Will you want something for dinner?' Pam asked, brushing a loose strand of black hair from her cheek and tucking it back behind her ear.

'Trial might go on all day,' Calvin explained. 'I wouldn't do anything special.'

He stood up and checked his appearance in a mirror that hung over the brick fireplace. His eyes dropped to the high waxed collar and black tie framed by the V of his black vest. He felt uncomfortable, for he preferred his collars open, and his hair hanging loose and not slicked down as it was now.

'You look handsome, Calvin.' Pam let him know how impressed she was.

'I feel a freak,' Calvin admitted. 'This is not me.'

Pam came behind him and placed her hands, gently, on his shoulders. Calvin stared at her reflection, at her square face with its full-lipped smile, pert nose and laughing brown eyes, all framed by waves of shining black hair. She was, he had to agree, everything a man could want in a woman.

'Better get to work,' he said abruptly, unable to keep a thickness from his voice.

'Good luck,' Pam called after him as he left the dining-room at a brisk pace.

Once outside he allowed himself to slow down and wave at Jed Farley who was almost running down the street to his home. He looked around, exchanged greetings with passers-by and in no time he was swinging into his office.

'Any trouble?' he asked of Phelan who was lounging by the cells.

Phelan shook his head. 'I ain't got no troubles. Colby has a problem, though. Nothin' that breakfast won't cure.'

'Breakfast's at nine,' Calvin stated,

sitting down behind his desk. 'You know the routine.'

Phelan did not bother to acknowledge, instead he busied himself with his makings and rolled himself a cigarette.

Promptly, at nine o'clock, the fifty-year-old spinster, Molly Fairbrother, who helped out Pam Ross in the kitchen, came over to the jailhouse with breakfast for the prisoners.

'What have they got today, Molly?' Calvin asked, as Molly set the double-stacked trays on his desk and removed the top one.

'Beans and eggs,' Molly stated, removing two red checked towels so that the lawman could see for himself.

'Beans,' groaned Colby from his cell. 'Don't you have nothin' else?'

'You don't get a menu here,' Calvin retorted. 'Just be grateful you get fed. Folks around here think otherwise after what happened to Sam Vennor.'

'Well, he should've worn a badge,'

Colby countered. 'Then we'd've known what he was.'

Calvin did not respond. That was the weakness in that part of the case. Sam had been drinking when MacGrath and his men had walked in. No doubt believing that he was doing his duty, he had pulled his gun and gone to arrest them. They had gunned him down. It was that simple—and conceivable that a plea of self-defence would be acceptable.

'Serve them,' Calvin said to Molly his tone harsher than he meant it to be.

Molly did as she was told and seven of the men thanked her. Only Colby felt that he had cause to complain.

'You know, lady,' he grumbled, 'I'm gettin' so I hate the sight of beans. If I had the chance—'

'Enough,' Abel MacGrath intervened. 'No need to vent your spleen on this lady. She's done you no harm. You want to carry on then you'll have to settle with me.'

Colby threw a sneer at Molly, then lurched back to his mattress where he sat down and ate his breakfast.

'Thank you,' Molly said, looking shyly at the rugged man who had come to her aid.

MacGrath shook his head. 'Save your thanks, lady. We've done the damage by letting him have his head. 'Sides if one of us hadn't stepped in the lawman there would've done.'

'You're a strange man, Abel MacGrath,' Molly observed. 'You are as you are, but I get the feeling—'

'Don't have feelin's, lady,' MacGrath interrupted. 'At least not for the likes of me. I am what I am and there's no changin' that. Born to hang is what I've allus figured.'

'I don't believe that,' Molly stated, a little defeated. 'And I don't think you do, either. I'll just respect your wishes and say nothing more.'

'Thank you, lady,' MacGrath acknowledged. 'And for the breakfast, too.'

He watched her walk away with a sense of regret. Another time, another place—if there had been a woman like her. If. The word rang inside his head. The truth was that there never had been anyone like her, not when he had needed her. So, instead, he had ridden the trail to this point in time.

'Reckon old Abel's in love,' Colby commented.

'Oh, shut up,' Deke Tinsley snapped. 'You say another word and I'll be taking work away from the hangman.'

The jailhouse became unusually silent now that Colby's voice could not be heard. With it came the nervous tension of men waiting for the long walk to the courthouse. Even a promise of freedom was not enough for the prisoners for they knew that they still had to face a hostile crowd.

When Jed Farley returned, the prisoners were released in pairs and handcuffed together. All this while Calvin unlocked the gun cabinet behind the desk and removed three sawn-down shot-guns which he loaded. He handed one to Cliff Phelan and another to Jed when the deputy had finished with the prisoners.

'Let me make one thing clear,' Calvin addressed the prisoners, as he opened the door of the jailhouse. 'Anyone who thinks of making a run for it—we shoot. These shot-guns have a wide spread, so be sure we can get two of you for the price of one.'

'Ain't none of us goin' to run,' Abel MacGrath promised.

'Obliged for your word,' Calvin acknowledged, then jerked his head at Phelan. 'Take the point, Cliff. Jed keep back at the rear and don't let your nerves get the better of you.'

Abel MacGrath and Deke Tinsley followed Phelan out of the jailhouse, and once outside the prisoners began to march down the street. They held their heads high with a sense of misplaced pride.

Like soldiers, Calvin thought. Then dismissed the whole idea as he moved down to cover their flank.

'Murderers,' someone in the gathering crowd yelled.

Phelan swivelled around, the shot-gun thrust out in front of him.

'Easy boy,' MacGrath cautioned.

'Just an insult,' Tinsley told him, easily. 'If there were anything more, one of us would be dead by now.'

Phelan grimaced as he relaxed a little, though resentful that it took a bunch of killers to advise him how to calm his nerves. Then he wished that he had stayed alert as a youngster came charging out of an alleyway with a rifle thrust out at waist level.

'Get clear, Phelan,' the youth warned.

'No, Jason,' Calvin spoke with authority, as he veered around to stand in front of Phelan.

Jason Vennor, the dead deputy's seventeen-year-old son, stood there resolute.

'Don't stop me,' Jason pleaded. 'You know what they did to my pa. You know what they will say.'

'I know they killed your pa,' Calvin agreed, taking a soft pace closer to the youngster. 'And they will hang. Just as you will if you kill one of them.'

While Jason looked about him seeking support from the crowd, Calvin closed the distance between them. But he was not fast enough, for a big man in a grey pinstripe suit came from behind and cracked Jason behind the ear with the flat of his hand. Jason collapsed into the dusty street but the big man showed no concern as he snatched up the rifle.

For a moment Calvin locked eyes with the man and felt disturbed.

Thanks,' he said. 'I could've handled it.'

'I'm sure you could,' the big man responded, evenly.

Calvin nodded and walked backwards, signalling to Phelan to get the prisoners on the move again. When he glanced over at the crowd, the big man was not to be seen.

It was then that something triggered in Calvin's mind. He recalled the events of the day before and the conversation that he had overheard. He coupled that with the orderliness of the prisoners. He knew, right then, that they were going to walk free.

He looked back to where Jason Vennor was being lifted to his feet. Calvin felt a wave of guilt wash over him as he realized that not only would Jason feel let down but so would the whole town. If MacGrath and his men were acquitted, then he, Calvin, was finished.

Still preoccupied with his thoughts, it took him a moment or two to realize that they had come to the steps to the courthouse. Phelan was already opening the doors and directing the prisoners inside. Calvin stood to one side waiting for the entourage to pass by, then followed on behind Jed.

The prisoners filed into the bench behind the defence table, with Phelan sitting behind them. Jed his role completed, went back to the office to mind the shop.

From the prosecution table, Calvin watched the spectators pour in. The presence of two men began to bother him: Tunbridge and the big man in the grey suit, both men on either side of the aisle, with the big man at the back. The two acknowledged each other, but that was all. Enough for Calvin to know that something was going on that he did not like.

FOUR

The courtroom buzzed with speculation, making Calvin feel vulnerable and self-conscious which was heightened when the burly defence lawyer, Max Haymes, waddled over to offer a deal. The shooting of Sam Vennor was still a sticking point. The burden of proof lay on Cal showing that MacGrath and his men knew that Sam was a deputy. Haymes wanted Cal to drop the charge.

Cal was adamant. There would be no deals. Haymes just shrugged and walked off, but the way he looked at the spectators only served to cause the lawman more concern.

Now it was time. The court bailiff was taking up his position by the door to the judge's chambers. The general buzz died away as the spectators settled down in expectation.

'All rise,' the bailiff intoned, sombrely, 'for his honour Judge John D. Cox.'

The judge entered the court, took his place and shuffled a bundle of papers in front of him, then looked up and nodded. Everyone sat, ready to listen to the evidence in the case of the People versus Abel MacGrath and others. They listened as the list of charges was read out.

Cox drummed his fingers on his desk top, his eyes gazing steadily at Cal as he rose to present his case.

'Gentlemen,' Cox called, before Calvin could get into his stride. 'I suggest you approach the bench.'

The portly defence lawyer, Max Haymes, and Calvin exchanged glances before doing what the judge had asked. Neither man betrayed any clue as to why they should be summoned to the bench.

Cox glared at Calvin. 'Are you seriously going to proceed with this case?'

Calvin nodded. 'I am. Unless you know something that I don't.'

The judge snorted and bit back the temptation to fine the lawman in contempt of court.

'I have read the evidence,' Cox reminded both men. 'What I find is that I have eight men before me accused of stealing cattle; a hired hand was shot attempting to prevent the theft. There is no evidence to show that these eight men were involved in either offence. I concede that they were in possession of the cattle at the time of their arrest. However, these men did have a bill of sale which, we know, was not signed by the legitimate owner. I have to say that the case against them is sparse and too circumstantial.

'Now we have Sam Vennor, a deputized law enforcement officer who does not wear his official badge nor does he make his position known to these eight men. He enters a saloon where the defendants are drinking. He does this with a drawn gun and proceeds to make an arrest. In fact most of the affidavits state that he said, "You scum are coming with me". There is an offensive interchange between all the parties concerned. Vennor fires his gun into the air, perhaps, as a warning. Someone—'

'Self-defence,' Max Haymes stated. 'I agree with Your Honour's form of reasoning. This would have been the case for the defence. I beg Your Honour to dismiss this case.'

'Perhaps, Mr Nicholls would like to say something,' Cox invited, 'There may be something that I have missed.'

'Do I have a choice?' Calvin asked, bitterly, his eyes holding those of the judge.

For a moment Cox looked frightened, then looked away, to quickly compose himself.

'Everyone has a choice,' Cox assured him. 'Sometimes there are no alternatives. In this case I would advise that you accede to the defence's plea. To proceed further could prove costly as I have the power to dismiss the case at any time.'

'Those men are guilty as charged,' Calvin protested.

'Prove it,' challenged Haymes.

Calvin knew that he could not. Not in court. He glanced at the jury, twelve men waiting to deliver a pre-ordained guilty vote. Calvin saw bias in every face. Sam Vennor was dead and, as far as they were concerned, eight men were going to hang for it. And he, Calvin, wanted them to die, too.

Calvin sighed, resignedly. 'I leave it to you, Your Honor. You make the decision.'

Calvin returned to his desk and slumped into his chair. He was too preoccupied with his thoughts to hear the case dismissed and ignored the pandemonium that followed when Abel MacGrath and his men walked free.

As he was to tell Pam Ross later that day, he felt that his world had collapsed about him. Everyone knew that Sam Vennor had been gunned down in cold blood, just as they knew about the stolen cattle and the death of the hired hand. Knowing was one thing, but proving it was quite another.

To add insult to injury, Jed Farley had walked up to him and slammed his badge down on the table.

'Sam was a friend,' he said. 'I can't believe that you let them fellas go free without a fight.'

Calvin did not have it in him to argue the point. Right then, he could have quite happily, quit the job himself.

He stood up and glanced at the bailiff, who beckoned to him. Calvin went over to find out what he wanted. The bailiff just glared at him and opened the door to the judge's chambers.

Calvin took the hint and went in.

'I am sorry,' Cox blurted out.

'Not good enough,' Calvin fired back. 'You lied to me. What I want to know is why should a man like Major Tunbridge want those men freed?'

'I do not know the answer to that,' Cox stated. 'What I do know is this: I had orders direct from the President himself to do what was necessary. I do not like it any more than you do, but it is done now. I doubt if it will be any consolation to you, but my role as a judge ended when I acquitted those men.'

'At least you're not in debt anymore,' Calvin rasped with disgust.

'I have no debts,' the judge admitted. 'I never had debts. Bribery, Calvin, only works when a man has a weakness that others can exploit. In my case, I used debt. It was the right bait, although I find the whole business quite obnoxious. Of one thing I am grateful: that is that you overheard the conversation as did another gentleman. You will both be my witnesses.'

Calvin gave the judge a long look. Everything that was being said was adding to his confusion.

'All right, Cox,' he demanded, all etiquette forgotten in his growing fury, 'why don't you just tell me what is going on here?'

The judge hesitated, then said, 'I do not really know any more than I have already told you.'

'But you know who can,' Calvin prompted.

'Willard Dull,' the judge replied. 'He is the government man. Big man. You cannot miss him. Sandy hair. Wears grey pinstriped city suits. Find him and, perhaps, you will get your answers.'

Calvin allowed the brief description to sink in. His memory filled in the picture. It was the man who had disarmed Jason Vennor. And that man had also been in court.

'I think I know who you mean,' Calvin acknowledged, thoughtfully.

'I hope you do not think too badly of me,' the judge said, sadly.

'No change in my opinion, Cox,' Calvin

stated sharply, wanting the other to know exactly how he felt. 'No matter what, you served this town badly.'

Judge Cox sighed. 'Calvin. Let me tell you something. Forget Tunbridge. Forget Dull. What I said today, in court, I stand by. The evidence, as it stood, was flimsy. You could have put every witness you had on the stand and a good defence lawyer would show two things: one, bias, because Sam was a respected member of the community; two, self-defence, because of the way Sam carried out his duty. There was no need for bribery or coercion. The case you had was precarious to say the least.'

'The jury would have—' Calvin started to protest.

'Found them all guilty,' the judge finished for him. 'A biased jury would have returned that verdict. You know that. Max Haymes knew that. Either one of you could have made a plea for a new venue and an impartial jury. Neither of you wanted to do that. You because you wanted the conviction: Haymes because his clients were going to be acquitted. I trust that you see that not all the blame can be laid at my feet.'

Calvin glared at the judge, then turned away. He felt bitter at the accusation but recognized the truth in it.

'What about you?' he asked at length. 'Folks'll be getting themselves into a fuss over this.'

'I agree,' the judge replied. 'I think it would be prudent if I left town right away.'

'There's a train at noon,' Calvin reminded him.

'I will be on it,' Judge Cox promised.

'I'll have my deputy stay with you,' Calvin offered. 'At least you'll have some protection. Come train time we'll both escort you to the station.'

'You have my gratitude,' the judge smiled, then offered his hand. 'I hope that there are no hard feelings. It would be a pity if our relationship was marred by this one mess.'

Calvin shook hands. 'Time'll sort it all out, I guess. Some sense will come from all this.'

'Just watch out for Dull,' the judge cautioned. 'I believe that he could be a dangerous man.'

'Maybe,' Calvin admitted. 'Once you're on that train both he and Tunbridge become my concern.'

While Calvin was spending time with the judge, he missed something that would have caused him greater concern.

Major Samuel Tunbridge stood on the court steps, watching the eight men enter the livery stable at the end of the street. He lit a long, slim cigar and blew out a satisfied streamer of smoke. Yet, despite his easy manner, he was uneasy.

'Well, they are free men for now, Tunbridge,' the soft voice startled him.

Tunbridge turned to look into those

almost innocent looking blue eyes; eyes that could go cold and hard in an instant. Willard Dull's eyes. And the past became very prominent in the present.

'You cannot touch any of us, now, Dull,' he said, forcefully. 'The Statute of Limitations expired eleven months ago. You cannot hang us for things that happened in the war.'

'What about the things you've done since?' Dull asked, conversationally.

'How else were we supposed to live?' Tunbridge fired back. 'We could not settle down and earn an honest living. Those who tried are dead.'

'What do you expect?' Dull's tone was innocent.

'We are the ones being hounded,' Tunbridge pointed out. 'But the orders came from you.'

'There is no proof,' Dull smiled. 'All records are destroyed. What is left are people's memories. And an investigation by Senator Lucius Guest into the murder of his son by Federal troops.'

Tunbridge looked thoughtful for a moment. 'What happened at Mansfield was an act of war. We attacked an ammunition supply dump and destroyed it. In accordance with orders: *your* orders, Dull.'

'Which came from the President himself,' Dull reminded him, in a statement that seemed to exonerate him from all blame. 'There was nothing in those orders that said you had the right to kill prisoners of war.'

Tunbridge took a draw on his cigar. 'Dull, you know that is the one thing you did not tell us. That there were Federal prisoners of war being held there. We were in a kill or be killed situation. The only uniforms that we saw were grey. Anyway why should this senator still want to rake it up now? You hanged Crandell for a scapegoat.'

'Captain Marcus Guest,' Dull explained, evenly. 'The senator's son, was one of the men you killed. Senator Lucius is one dogged man who does not intend to rest until every one of his son's killers is dead. Justice, Major Tunbridge, has to be seen to be done. The good senator knows the names of those who are still alive. He has a convincing dossier of evidence. The Department has commissioned me to close the case.'

'So shoot,' Tunbridge invited. 'You will not have a better opportunity.'

Dull shook his head. 'Not this time. Like I said, justice must be seen to be done. You cannot be charged with the Mansfield massacre, but you are the brains behind a series of robberies.'

'Really?' Tunbridge asked with mock surprise.

'Really,' Dull chuckled. 'Next to me you were the best planner in the Department. What does amaze me is that you chose to ride with Crandell on this particular mission.'

'Planning is one thing,' Tunbridge said,

seriously. 'What I really wanted was action. I wanted to see for myself what all our planning achieved.'

'The worst thing you could have done,' Dull commiserated.

'Depends,' Tunbridge shrugged. 'All that matters now is that those who are left survive—by any means possible.'

'You sound determined,' Dull mentioned.

'Because we were once colleagues,' Tunbridge offered, 'I will give you until the noon train tomorrow to leave town. From that moment on, the gloves will be off—you won't live to see the case closed.'

Dull nodded, sagely. 'I take your point. I will give your offer consideration. However, let me inform you that the Department gets a weekly report. If I die someone will take my place.'

'Goodbye, Willard,' Tunbridge said, with finality.

'For now, Sam, for now,' Dull promised. He stood for a while watching Tunbridge stroll up the street. For all his complacency, Dull felt a touch of worry. It was as though he knew that all his careful planning was going to end in tragedy.

Calvin left the judge's chambers to find Cliff Phelan still in the courtroom.

'What are you doing here?' Calvin demanded.

Startled, Phelan could only stammer out, 'L-looking for you.'

'Why?' Calvin persisted.

Phelan shrugged, thinking that he could use a truth to explain his presence. 'The office was getting a little overcrowded. Lot of people want to talk to you.'

Calvin threw him a rueful look, then grinned. 'Better go and face them. It's not an unexpected situation.' He jerked a thumb at the judge's chambers. 'His Honour is leaving town. Give him some protection until I get back.'

'Don't worry,' Phelan acknowledged. 'I'll take care of him.'

He waited until Calvin had gone before going to the door on which he knocked before entering.

Calvin threaded his way through a crowd of people who fired questions at him all at once. In such a small room the cacophony ricochetted from the walls making it sound as though the whole town was crammed in.

Calvin called for calm but his voice was drowned. Everyone was asking questions and did not want to hear the answers. Silence only came when he drew his gun and fired it at the ceiling.

'Everybody out,' Calvin roared, aiming the barrel of his gun at the crowd. 'Then send back three men to act as your spokesmen: one to use his mouth; the others to use just their ears.'

Mayor Ferguson thrust his thin frame forward. 'You can't speak to me like that.'

'One more word out of you,' Calvin retorted, angrily, 'and I'll arrest you for causing a breach of the peace—and that goes for the rest of you.'

Some were ready to protest, but changed their minds when they realized that the lawman meant every word he said. Slowly, grudgingly, the crowd began to disperse and it was some ten minutes later that three men came back in.

Mayor Ferguson had been joined by Major Tunbridge and another town councillor, Frank Bridge.

'We feel that we are owed an explanation,' Ferguson snapped, in a nasal voice.

'Too right,' Frank Bridge echoed.

'You spokesmen or listener, Frank?' Calvin asked, politely.

'Keep quiet, Frank,' Ferguson admonished.

'Right. Ask your questions,' Calvin invited.

'MacGrath and his men went free today,' Ferguson stated. 'What do you have to say about that.'

Calvin sat down, hooked his bootheels

against the edge of his desk and tilted his chair back on to its rear legs.

'A travesty of justice,' Calvin put in bluntly. 'The evidence was there but it wasn't enough. When it came down to it—well—Frank you were there.' Bridge nodded. 'Sam wasn't wearing a badge and he went up to them with a drawn gun. Did he tell them who he was?'

'Jus' told them they was under arrest,' Bridge admitted. 'Wanted for cattle rustlin' and killin'. Then they jus' gunned him down.'

'Did they know what Sam did in this town?' Calvin asked, then seeing Bridge's frown of confusion. 'Did they know that Sam was a deputy?'

'How the hell should I know?' Bridge demanded. 'Never seen any of them fellas before.'

Ferguson glared at his fellow councillor. 'You can't say that. You sound like a man making a case for self-defence.'

'Exactly,' stated Tunbridge.

'Same as everyone else would who saw Sam gunned down,' Calvin expanded, looking directly at Tunbridge. 'The judge had already read the evidence and it was the conclusion he had come to.'

Frank Bridge may have been slow in some things, but in this instance he came to the right conclusion. 'So even had we said our piece, we'd've got them off?'

'That's about the size of it,' Calvin acknowledged. 'But don't take my word for it. Go talk to the judge.'

'I do not think that will be necessary,' Tunbridge said, a touch hastily. 'I think Calvin here, has made the point quite clear.'

Ferguson looked as though he wanted to say something; more to assert his position than anything else. Instead he remained quiet, his time would come when he addressed the people waiting outside.

One by one the delegation left the office. Tunbridge paused at the door.

'What will you do now?' he asked.

'I don't know, I haven't decided,' Calvin stated. 'Why? What do you want me to do?'

Tunbridge shrugged. 'Just interested. I want you to do whatever you choose to do. Stay or go. I have no intention of influencing you.'

Calvin swallowed back his impulse to reveal to Tunbridge what he knew about the bribe.

Instead said, 'I'm glad of that.'

Tunbridge just smiled and nodded, then went out to mingle with the crowd.

Calvin tipped the chair forward and swung his legs back to the floor. It was time to go and relieve Phelan and escort the judge to the station. He was almost down to the courthouse when the first shot rang out.

'I'm to stay with you,' Phelan explained his presence to the judge who was busy packing away his lawbooks into a Gladstone bag.

'Yes, I know,' the judge replied, distracted by what he was doing.

'Mind if I open the window?' Phelan asked. 'Kinda stuffy in here.'

'As you wish,' the judge stated, with a negligent wave of his hand.

Phelan moved to the window and shoved the lower sash upwards.

He leaned a buttock on the sill and watched the judge finish his packing and lock up his bag.

'Guess you'll be glad to see the back of this place,' Phelan was making conversation, something to fill in the time.

'You, probably, feel like the rest about my decision,' the judge suggested, tiredly. 'I let guilty men go free.'

'You did what you had to,' Phelan mused, sliding his gun from its holster. 'You know, Sam was a good sort. I liked him. Just because I'm a youngster, you know, he never talked down to me. None of that older and wiser stuff most fellas spill out.'

'I know what you mean,' the judge agreed. 'That is why I hate myself for the decision I made.'

'Tough old world, ain't it,' Phelan said, grimly, as he pulled the trigger and shot the judge through the back of his head.

He watched the old man collapse on to the table, down which he slid leaving a red trail in his wake. Only when he had slumped to the floor did Phelan turn around and lean out of the window.

'Hey,' he yelled, then fired two shots into the wall of the building opposite.

This done, he swung out of the window and dropped to the dirt track below and set off at a run up the alley, to burst out into the main street as though he was chasing someone and collided with Calvin. Both men went down in a heap, but quickly untangled themselves. Phelan was the first to his feet, all the while looking around him as though searching for a fugitive.

'What the hell—' Calvin roared, dusting himself down.

'Judge Cox,' Phelan panted, bending down to retrieve his dropped revolver. 'Somebody just shot him.' He glanced around at the gathering crowd. 'I took a couple of shots at him. Figure I missed. Saw him run out into the street. You should've seen him.'

'Well, I didn't,' Calvin snapped. 'Did you get to see who it was?'

Phelan bit his lip, his eyes dropping to the ground. 'Jason Vennor.'

'You sure of that?' Calvin asked, as the name passed through the crowd.

'Positive,' Phelan replied, firmly.

FIVE

Jason Vennor.

As good a scapegoat as any, Calvin thought. The boy had a good motive for he must have felt let down by the judge's decision. He could, also, have been hot-headed enough to have made an impulsive killing.

'Right,' Calvin decided. 'You'd best find Jason and lock him up. Make sure you stay with him. Folks may have not agreed with what the judge did today, but they respect him just the same. There's always those belligerent enough to try for a lynching.'

Phelan nodded. He was only too grateful to be away from the lawman for a while.

Calvin proceeded to the courthouse and entered the judge's chambers. He took careful note of where the judge had fallen, then made some rapid deductions. Later he could get confirmation of his thoughts from his deputy.

Having made a careful study of the room, he climbed through the window and dropped into the alley below. He recalled the scuff marks on the window sill and the deep heel marks in the dirt. No doubt caused by Phelan taking the same route earlier. He allowed himself a wry smile as he noted that Phelan was heavy on his heels, the way they tracked through the dirt towards the main street. If he needed evidence that Phelan had fired at something, then two fresh scars showed in the boarded side of the opposite building.

He walked back to the open window and looked up, his lips pursed as something odd occurred to him. He frowned as he paced backwards and forwards between the two buildings, his eyes fixed in the gap in the open window. Something was wrong with Phelan's story.

As he walked back up the alley, he saw Major Tunbridge standing prominently in the middle of the street. He was in earnest conversation with a group of people who included the mayor and Bridge. On seeing the lawman approach, Tunbridge excused himself.

'What happened?' Tunbridge asked, his voice low and concerned.

'The judge was paid off,' Calvin snarled. 'And we both know why.'

Tunbridge raised his eyebrows, adopting a look of innocence. 'You should have listened to the judge. Where is your evidence for such an accusation.'

'I'll find it, Tunbridge,' Calvin snarled. 'Believe me, I will find it.'

'I do not think so,' Tunbridge challenged with a smile that did not touch his eyes. 'All the same, I wish you luck.'

Calvin just glared at the man, then turned on his heel and walked away. He called on the undertaker to take care of the corpse. Then headed back to the office where he found a sullen Jason Vennor behind bars.

The youngster threw himself at the bars as soon as Calvin entered. 'I din' do it, Mr Nicholls. I never killed that judge, honest.'

Calvin pursed his lips and studied the frightened boy; then said, 'Settle down, Jason. For the time being you're here for your own protection. Tempers are high out there, right now. You'll stay here until I get to the bottom of things.'

'But I din' do it,' Jason persisted.

Calvin did not reply. He just watched the youngster until Jason slumped, despondently, on to the lower bunk. Only then did Calvin leave, heading back to his desk where Phelan was resting a buttock on one corner.

'Right, Cliff,' Calvin sighed, sitting down and watching Phelan. 'Let's talk about the judge. What happened?'

Phelan told his version to which Calvin listened without interruption. To all intents and purposes it sounded plausible. Still, Calvin got Phelan to go through it all again and had to admit that there was no variation on the original story.

'How come the window was open?' Calvin asked.

'I did that,' Phelan admitted. 'Place was a bit stuffy.'

'Convenient,' Calvin confessed. 'Now where was Jason?'

'Didn't know he was there,' Phelan stated, frowning. 'Least not until I heard the gunshot. Guess he was in the middle of the alley when I saw him. By then he was running.'

Calvin nodded. 'You know you have one bad habit? It's the way you perch on things. Desks. Like right now, with your right boot pressed up against the desk leg.' He saw concern touch Phelan's face, then fade to be replaced by nonchalance. 'A little thing really, but it is a detail. That's what I want from you—a little more detail.'

'Can't think of anything else,' Phelan shrugged.

'Where were you in the room?' Calvin prompted. 'What could you see?'

Phelan looked at the ceiling as though to draw inspiration. 'Well, I was over in one corner, by a cupboard. Anyway there was a door there. I was leaning against it. The judge was in front of me. Well, he was side on, I guess.'

'Could you see out of the window?' Calvin pressed on.

'Some,' Phelan stated. 'Didn't see Jason though, not until he killed the judge and ran up the alley.'

Calvin nodded, thoughtfully.

'Well, I guess I got all I need to know,' he said after a deliberate pause. 'At least no lawyer's going to challenge your story.' Phelan smiled, grateful that he was in the clear. 'Best you get going now. Take a break. We've had a long day. Be back by six, so I can go and get my supper.'

'Obliged.' Phelan was genuinely pleased

at being given time off. 'See you at six.'

He slid off the edge of the desk and ambled out of the office.

With the deputy gone, Calvin picked up the key to Vennor's cell. He unlocked the door and sat down beside the trembling boy.

'You heard it all?' Calvin asked.

Jason Vennor nodded. 'He'll have me hang.'

'No he won't,' Calvin assured him. 'Tell me about yourself. Pick up the story from when you were disarmed.'

Jason Vennor could not remember much about what happened immediately after he had tried to shoot Abel MacGrath. Just that he was half-conscious and woke up fully on the bed over at Charlie Stanford's Emporium. Charlie had kept a regular check on the boy before closing up his store to take Jason home, by which time they both knew that his father's killers had been set free. Charlie would have stayed, but he had to get back and reopen his store.

'You could've followed him back,' Calvin stated, ruefully.

'Yes, but I didn't,' Jason protested, almost in tears. 'Besides I was home when that deputy of yours came to arrest me.'

Calvin patted the boy, reassuringly, on the shoulder. 'Figure that puts you in the clear. I know Charlie Stanford will back your story. And Phelan will confirm where he picked you up.' Then he became serious. 'For your own safety, I'm going to keep you here. Emotions are running high out there and I don't want you caught up in it. You understand me?'

Jason nodded. 'Thanks for believing me.'

Calvin just smiled and left the boy alone. He did not bother to lock the cell behind him. The boy would not be stupid enough to try and leave.

Willard Dull had spent some of the

afternoon talking to one or two people, but spent most of the time listening to the talk around town. For, only by listening, did he learn the things that would make his job easier. He discovered that despite one failure, Calvin Nicholls was well respected as was Major Tunbridge.

It was by listening that Dull added to his store of information on Tunbridge. Besides his interests in Summerhill, he owned property and land down in Oakridge as well. He had among his assets an abattoir and a freighting company, a stockyard and a medium-sized ranch. He also owned leases on several prosperous properties. Dull knew where the money had come from which was turning him into a wealthy and influential man. Yet, Dull had to consider, if Tunbridge was growing financially stronger what, then, of MacGrath and the others? It was they who robbed the stagelines, the trains and rustled cattle to support Tunbridge's quest for power. Why did they take the risks? he wondered. Surely, not out of loyalty.

Survival. The word hit Dull like a hammer blow, as he recalled his earlier conversation with Tunbridge. MacGrath and the others were still doing what they had trained to do in war and continuing into the peace. They were striking back at an enemy that wanted nothing more to do with them. All the while Major Tunbridge was giving them security and support in the only way he knew how.

For a moment Dull had to admire Tunbridge. He was looking after men who had served their country only to be treated as outcasts as soon as they were no longer needed.

Then Dull sobered. The way that they achieved things was by criminal acts which could not continue unpunished. He had a job to do and he had to bring it to a conclusion, no matter what his own personal feelings were.

The only way for him to bring matters to a head was to get the co-operation of the local lawman. From what Dull had seen and heard, he knew that Calvin Nicholls was no one to fool with—the kind of man who ranked alongside others like, Hickcock, Earp or Masterson, men to whom their badge meant something. Law, order and justice—sometimes in that order. Nicholls was strong on justice, which gave Dull the angle to work on.

He went to his room to retrieve the rifle he had taken from Jason Vennor. Then hastened over to the town marshal's office.

Laying the rifle on the desk he waited, patiently, until Nicholls finished writing up a report which Dull read upside down without appearing to do so.

'What can I do for you, Mr Dull?' Calvin asked as he scooped up the papers, opened a drawer and thrust them inside.

If Dull was surprised at the use of his name, he did not show it.

'The rifle I took off that boy,' Dull said, pointing at the rifle. 'I thought that I had better hand it over to you.'

'Thank you,' Calvin acknowledged, then with hardly any change in his expression, 'so why is the Government interested in Major Tunbridge and a bunch of outlaws?'

Dull stroked his chin, thoughtfully. His mind was thinking through things rather rapidly. It was one thing to shrug off recognition but another to be asked direct about information that the lawman should not have known. Only one way; he decided to skirt the issue.

'That boy did not kill judge Cox, you know,' Dull stated, matter-of-factly, staring towards the cells.

'I know that.' Calvin was blunt in his retort.

'I would be interested in what you know,' Dull mentioned, hooking a chair over with the toe of his boot and sitting down across from Calvin.

'Angle of the bullet, for one thing,' Calvin told him. 'Mark of a bootheel on the wall beneath the window. Just a couple of things. What about you? What can you add?'

'You are one hell of an intelligent man,' Dull had to admit. 'But what makes you think that I could add anything?'

Calvin laughed at the compliment, but it cut no ice with him.

'You've been to the scene of the crime,' Calvin pointed out. 'You've been over to the funeral parlour and looked over the corpse. And you read my report while I was writing it. So have we both drawn the same conclusion or do you have something to add?'

For the first time Dull felt uncomfortable. He shifted, uneasily, in the chair, resisting the temptation to get up and pace about.

'No one came out of that alley ahead of your deputy,' Dull admitted. 'I know, because I was directly opposite on the other side of the street when I heard the first shot.'

Calvin nodded. 'Thank you, Mr Dull.

For once, I have an eyewitness who can clear Jason Vennor. The evidence I had put Jason at home at the time of the killing. Not conclusive because it was feasible, though unlikely, that he could've returned to town in time to shoot Cox.'

Dull stood up. 'Well, I am glad I could be of assistance. Next time I go snooping around I think I will have to be a little more discreet.'

'Change your clothes, as well,' Calvin smiled. 'City suits tend to stick out. That's how I identified you when you walked in.'

Dull stroked his chin again and pursed his lips. 'It explains how you recognized me but as I told no one my name—'

'The judge told me who you were,' Calvin stated. 'Which brings me back to my original question before you tried to sidetrack me: what is your interest in Tunbridge and MacGrath?'

'They rode together in the war,' Dull confided. 'So did Royce who acts as a shotgun guard at that gambling saloon; Amos Biggelow, Tunbridge's bodyguard; and a man called Lou Phelan, whose son is your deputy. No need to worry about Lou, he is dead. But it makes you think does it not?'

Calvin nodded. 'It explains why Tunbridge bribed Cox.' Then quickly explained, 'I overheard them talking and I challenged them both on it. On the face of it they all served together, so I guess Tunbridge wanted MacGrath and the others released out of some kind of loyalty. As to the others, Royce and Biggelow, well, he gave them jobs.'

'And Phelan?' Dull prompted.

'That was down to me,' Calvin admitted, almost challenging Dull to comment on his judgement; then shrugged. 'The town council would only pay for one more deputy. Guess they did that to shut me up because I was making too much noise about needing more deputies. Then along came Phelan.'

Dull raised a quizzical eyebrow. 'Coincidence?'

Calvin stiffened. He felt that there was more behind the casual question than met the eye. Dull was seeking information.

'Maybe,' Calvin shrugged.

Dull nodded, thoughtfully. He was dealing with an intelligent man who had seen something in his, seemingly, innocent question. So he decided to try another tack.

'MacGrath and his gang are wanted in several States,' he commented. 'Why do you suppose, did they come to Summerhill to rustle some cattle and reduce the number of your deputies by one?'

'I'm sure you know the answer to that,' Calvin threw back, getting a bit fed up with this cat and mouse form of questioning.

Dull sighed and shifted his weight. 'I wish I did. Not even a suspicion. I hoped that you might have been able to shed some light on the matter.'

Calvin shook his head. 'You can't con

me, mister. You know more than what you're letting on. All you want from me is confirmation that you are on the right track. So how about a little more two-way conversation?'

For a moment, Dull, looked as though he was going to lose his temper. Then he visibly relaxed.

'Very well,' Dull stated. 'I will give you a piece of information and then I will ask a question. It has been known that at one time, MacGrath hired out his guns to settle some land disputes. They do not come cheap, but they do a quick and efficient job. Now, this man Brixham—the man whose cattle were stolen—was he in dispute with anyone?'

'Not that I know of,' Calvin admitted. 'When I checked up with him he had nothing to say about trouble.'

Dull smiled. 'Maybe you nipped it in the bud.'

Calvin frowned.

'What I mean is,' Dull supplied, 'you

caught MacGrath before any trouble could start.'

'Maybe,' Calvin mused, then stabbed an accusing finger at the government man. 'What I need to know is who would benefit? No one that I can think of.'

Dull stood up. 'I think that if we go any further we will be into the realms of speculation.'

'It'll have to remain a mystery,' Calvin said standing up, taking an instant dislike at the way Dull used both his height and position to talk down to people.

'But one that you and I are going to solve,' Dull suggested, with authority. 'Believe it or not, we are going to need to work together if we are to bring MacGrath and his men to book.'

'You need my help?' Calvin almost laughed out loud. 'Don't think I'm taken in. The way I figure it, you know a lot more than I do. And you have no intention of parting with any of it; or at least more than you have to.'

Dull threw him a shrewd glance. 'That is my way. I promise you, I will tell you all that you need to know—later. I will meet you here at nine tonight—make sure you are alone.'

It sounded strange, as he told Pam Ross over supper. She had been attentive as he had talked through mouthfuls of food.

'One thing you should've asked,' Pam pointed out, pouring him a cup of fresh coffee, 'was why he insisted the judge took the bribe.'

'Thought of it,' Calvin confessed. 'Somehow, I felt that it would've given Dull the idea that I knew a lot more than I do.' He cupped his hand around the cup and allowed the warmth of the contents to soak into his palms. 'You know, if I wanted men stopped, then I would've let them get tried and hanged.' He shook his head. 'The more I think about it, Tunbridge has to be the one he's after. Apart from them all having served together in the army, there's nothing to link them.'

'He gets a cut,' Pam offered, collecting up the dirty dishes and carrying them over to the drainer. 'One lot carries out the robberies, and Tunbridge gets a cut. Now you know how he made his money and got where he is today.'

Calvin was about to laugh. It was a great idea, but it sounded too far-fetched. Then he thought through the statement, piecing little bits together until they produced a feasible picture.

'You know,' he murmured, 'you could be on to something there.'

'Well, there you go,' she chuckled. 'Where would you men be without a woman to work it all out for you.' Then she slapped him on the shoulder. 'I was only kidding.'

He gave her a long look, then nodded his head, speculatively. With a sigh he put down the empty cup and rose from the chair, the legs scraping the stone floor. The noise made Pam turn around.

'You off, then?' she asked, out of habit.

'Few things to tidy up,' he said. 'Be back about ten.'

'When you're ready,' she smiled. 'Take you time: I'll be waiting up.'

Pam would. She was never happy until she knew that all her lodgers were in so that she could lock up for the night.

Calvin strode out and stood on the porch. He breathed in the cooling night air that still carried a hint of warm dust in it. Outside, away from Pam, he could relax for she was no longer a distracting woman who made him conscious of his weakness.

Cliff Phelan sat alone in the crowded saloon nursing a lukewarm beer. Around him was the buzz of card players, the rattle of crap dice and the groans of those who lost at the wheel of fortune, none of which penetrated his world of isolation for he was a man with a lot on his mind. Killing a judge had been easy, but the next victim was not so easy. Anybody else—well, there was a problem when it came to a man he liked and respected. All he wanted to do was get it over and done with.

As he lifted the glass of amber liquid, a tall thin man sat down in front of him.

'You shouldn't be here, Cliff.' Despite the polite tone, there was firmness in the thin man's tone.

Phelan glanced into a pair of narrow, watchful grey eyes, shaded by the brim of a roll-sided stetson.

'Things on my mind,' Phelan confessed.

'You'll be missed.' The other nodded at the clock over the bar. 'Comin' up to eight.'

'I'll be there, Bryden,' Phelan tried to assure the bouncer.

'Your pa never waited 'til the last minute,' Bryden Royce pointed out. 'I'm goin' up to meet Abel; how about we take a walk together?'

Phelan looked from the soft-spoken man to the sawn-down shotgun holstered against his right thigh; the pistol grip butt polished with use. The barrels were nine inches long, but a long split in the leather holster enabled Royce to make a fast draw. And Royce was not slow in demonstrating his prowess to underline a point. So when Royce made a suggestion without turning it into a question, it was wiser to do as he said.

'Why not?' Phelan shrugged.

Royce stood up and picked up Phelan's beer then toasted, 'To the honour of the regiment.'

He took a long pull at the beer before he slammed it back down on the table. Then glared at the young, half-risen deputy, who was staring at him with open-mouthed surprise.

'One thing you don't know,' Royce stated, 'is about pride. I've seen men die for it. We're all that's left of a damn fine regiment. So you make sure you do your pa proud, boy.'

'I'll do what has to be done,' Phelan promised.

Royce just snorted and turned his back on the young deputy. As far as he was concerned, Phelan did not have the same kind of commitment that his father had had.

'We got a drunk already?' Calvin asked, as he entered the office. 'Or did you slip out for a drink?'

'Just came back from the saloon,' Phelan confessed, knowing that there was no point in lying.

'You know how I feel about that,' Calvin reminded him.

'Drink and duty don't go together,' the deputy responded, irritably. 'But then you ain't tryin' to reason through a problem.'

Calvin leaned against the wall as Phelan slumped into the chair in front of the desk.

'Want to talk it through?' Calvin offered. 'I'm a willing listener.'

Phelan shook his head. 'It can wait. The problem'll get solved.'

Calvin pushed himself away from the wall. 'Maybe,' he mused, turning towards the door, but glancing over his shoulder at a youngster who was more interested in making patterns in the dusty floor with the toe of his boot. 'Tell you, when I get back, you can quit for the night. Get yourself drunk or sorted out or both. What I really want from you is the truth about what you saw in the alley earlier today. Understand?'

Phelan nodded. Then said, tonelessly, 'Like I said, the problem'll get sorted.'

Calvin left him to it while he took his customary night walk around the town.

Abel MacGrath and his men dismounted outside the livery stable situated at the extreme edge of the north of town. The liveryman had already been taken care of, his unconscious body trussed up in the empty end stall with the four hundred pounds of solid body and bald head that comprised Amos Biggelow. The six feet six inch giant moved nimbly for his weight, coming down the aisle to help the others berth their mounts.

'Let's get it done,' Abel murmured, then nodded at the red-headed Mel Johnson. 'Keep a good eye on the liveryman. No need for folks to know we're around.'

Ten men left the livery, Royce joining them just as they made their exit, to walk in line abreast down the main street. They stopped outside the law office, the door of which opened to spill a wedge of light across the rutted road. Cliff Phelan approached the group, moving in front of them until he was alongside Abel MacGrath.

'No nerves?' Royce asked, innocently.

'Not now,' Phelan confessed. 'Got a reason, now.'

'Wait for me,' MacGrath growled. 'Don't be too hasty.'

The others drifted away, taking up positions along the boardwalk, unaware that their every move was being watched.

Pam Ross stood, spellbound, at her bedroom window. She glanced down the street and saw Calvin, slowly, approach his office. Fear rooted her to the spot, for she knew that even if she could move she would never warn Calvin in time.

Willard Dull was enjoying a good steak when he became conscious of a presence. With a forkful of steak poised halfway to his mouth, he looked up at Major Tunbridge who smiled as he pulled out a chair and sat down opposite the government man.

'I trust it will not spoil your appetite if I join you?' he asked, signalling to a black-trousered, white-shirted waiter. 'We have not had a chance to talk over old times.'

Dull slammed the piece of steak into his mouth and made an angry chewing sound.

Tunbridge gave his order, then addressed Dull, 'I hope you have bought your ticket for the noon train tomorrow.'

Dull shook his head. 'Threats do not

bother me. However, I concede this time. Just let me advise you, that you are going to hang one way or another.'

'Willard, you do not want me to die,' Tunbridge smiled. 'If I do hang, it will mean your demise and cause great embarrassment for the President.'

'Oh, come on, Sam,' Dull scoffed. 'You do not expect me to fall for that old story.'

'Do you recall how we planned our raids?' Tunbridge stated, seriously. 'We both made copies—what did we call it—our insurance, just in case.'

Dull felt the blood drain from his face and his mouth dry.

'We signed our copies, did we not?' Tunbridge continued, aware of the other's discomfort. 'Well, mine are in a very safe place. Today I gave instructions that on my death then my copies of the documents relating to the Mansfield fiasco be handed to Senator Lucius Guest.'

'You are bluffing, Sam,' Dull almost

roared to disguise his panic.

'Call it, Willard,' Tunbridge grinned. 'Call it and find out.'

The waiter came to the table, took a plate of steak and potatoes from a silver tray and set it before the self-assured Major.

'I will call it,' Dull growled, as the waiter moved away. 'I cannot allow you and your men to ride roughshod over this country carrying on as if the war never ended.'

'Your funeral,' Tunbridge shrugged, as he sliced a piece of steak and lifted the fork to his mouth. He chewed for a moment, then said, 'You know, this steak is really good. I get it fresh, you know.'

A testy remark sprang to Dull's lips, only to die as he shuddered and ducked as a fusillade of shots echoed down the street.

At first Calvin was only aware of the two shapes standing in the street, then one stepped forward and he recognized Abel MacGrath.

'Want you to know,' MacGrath said.

'No hard feelin's but I got a job to get done.'

Calvin did not get the chance to ask any questions, for MacGrath was already drawing his gun. Calvin acted fast, his gun clearing leather in time for him to trigger the first shot. Which took MacGrath in the chest rocking him. He tried to lift his gun, but the act produced an excruciating wave of pain that racked his body. His knees buckled and he fell to kneel at Calvin's feet. There was a pause during which Calvin looked from the almost dead MacGrath to the other shape.

'Best make your move,' Calvin challenged. 'Or ride out.'

His answer came from all sides as, belatedly, Phelan drew his gun, acting like a signal to the others to blast away. Shot-gun, rifle and revolver fire thundered against the fronts of buildings as Calvin's body was shredded and tossed about like a rag doll until he lay lifeless on the ground.

The shooting would have continued had not the dying Abel MacGrath been able to issue his last command.

'Ceasefire,' he yelled, hoarsely. 'He's dead. Now get out.'

Deke Tinsley stepped off the boardwalk, as the others beat a hasty retreat back to the livery. He laid a hand on MacGrath's shoulder.

'Leave me, Deke,' MacGrath panted. 'I'm out of it now.'

Having said his piece, MacGrath fell forwards to lay sprawled out.

Deke Tinsley walked away, sad at the loss of another comrade and renewing his vow of vengeance against a country that had deserted him.

As the shooting died away, Dull rose to his feet intending to join the other diners who were anxious to sate their curiosity.

'The town has just lost its lawman,' Tunbridge informed him, while still continuing with his meal. 'Shows you just what we can do, does it not?'

'You cold, callous bastard,' Dull spat, slowly sinking down into his chair.

'He knew too much,' Tunbridge shrugged. 'He was a threat to our survival. Just as you are.' He stabbed his knife at Dull to emphasize his words. 'Noon tomorrow, Willard, and you join Nicholls.' Then he smiled. 'No point in going to the law. My men will be holding office.'

Dull smiled, coldly. 'Well, at least, I'll know where to find them.'

The telegraph operator came bursting in waving a telegraph message.

'Major, I sure as hell don't know what to do,' he croaked, worriedly. 'Calvin's got hisself shot up and this message done come for him. Seems his pa's gone and died.'

Tunbridge shook his head, sadly. 'A bad day for the family. I think it would be wise to return the message. Perhaps, inform them that Calvin is also deceased.'

The telegraph operator ducked and

bowed and ran out of the dining-room.

'Such compassion,' Dull said, sarcastically. 'Invite the whole family up here to have a double burial.'

'There is no family,' Tunbridge stated, authoritatively. 'The only person Calvin ever talked about was his father.' He laughed. 'Do you know what his father was?' And, when Dull shook his head, 'An undertaker. Makes you wonder who will bury the dead.'

Dull pushed his half-eaten meal away from him and stood up.

'You have not finished,' Tunbridge pointed out.

'I have lost my appetite,' Dull snarled. 'Besides, if I am to be on the noon train, I had better get packed.'

'Thank you, Willard,' Tunbridge stated, genuinely. 'I would find it hard to live with your death on my conscience.'

Dull was about to make a retort, then thought better of it. For a moment he could see things from Tunbridge's side and knew that he would have acted no differently.

'From now on, Sam, we are enemies,' Dull assured him.

'I am sorry, Willard,' Tunbridge confessed with regret.

'No need to be,' Dull said. 'You are concerned for the survival of your men. Now you have made me concerned about my own survival.'

'Our lives are in each other's hands,' Tunbridge reminded him.

'Is that right?' Dull mocked. 'We shall see.'

He turned on his heel and walked away.

In the telegraph office the operator was busy wording a message to the sender of the telegraph that told of Nicholls senior's death. He did not know that he was about to trigger a series of events that would bring the man in black to Summerhill.

SIX

The sun was setting, a half disc of gold, behind the distant hills to the west as the man in black rode into town to halt outside the livery and dismount from the grey gelding. He unfastened a kite-shaped, canvas package that had covered his mount's left flank, and carried it over to rest against a corral pole. Then he returned to lead the horse inside the stable. As there was no one about, he led the horse into an empty stall where he removed the saddle, which he set down on the straw-covered floor so that he could detach the saddle gun and saddle-bags. Then lifted the saddle up on to the tree provided.

'Jist stay that way, mister.' The voice from behind him was harsh and dry.

The man in black did as he was told. His face was expressionless as he waited, patiently, for the next order.

'Now turn around, nice and slow.' The voice challenged him to do otherwise.

The man in black turned to see a man in his early forties and a good ten inches shorter than him, aiming a double-barrelled shot-gun, steadily, at him.

'Who are you?' the gun wielding man demanded.

'You don't want to know,' the man in black growled. 'Just want my horse stabled and fed while I attend to my business.'

The stableman lowered his shot-gun, just a fraction, but enough to remove an immediate threat to the stranger.

'Don't do to jist walk in an' do as you please,' he grumbled, not sure whether to give the stranger the benefit of the doubt.

'There was no one about,' the stranger stated, dropping his arms to his side.

'I'll attend to my business,' the stable-man said, shouldering the shot-gun. 'You get about yourn.'

The man in black gave the liveryman an ice-cold glare then turned on his heel and walked to the tall, open, double doors. Then he glared over his shoulder at the man who was busy attending to the horse.

'Obliged,' he growled, before stepping over to lift the canvas-wrapped package, which he hoisted up on to his shoulder before asking, 'The cemetery?'

The liveryman turned to him and called out, 'South end of town. You can't miss it. There's a white-painted church right alongside.'

The man in black walked down the main street; a darkness that seemed to blend with the lengthening shadows. By the time he reached the graveyard, the sun had disappeared behind the mountains leaving the sky a fiery red that held back the encroaching darkness.

It did not take him long to find the grave. He stared at the crude marker and scowled. All the deceased had got from the town was a cheap funeral.

The man in black, carefully almost reverently, laid the package alongside the grave. Then scooped the marker from its place and hurled it across the graveyard where it fell with a clatter after bouncing off a low brick wall, an action that did nothing to lessen the anger that he felt deep inside.

He knelt by the package and unfastened the ropes before spreading out the canvas that had covered a varnished wooden cross and a heart-shaped shovel. Picking up the latter, he began to dig deep into the the hard-packed earth. Only when the hole was big enough to accommodate half the shaft of the cross did he stop.

Placing the shovel to one side, he bent down to lift the cross, the shaft of which he set into the newly dug hole. He secured the base with rocks and stones, until the cross was perfectly set. Then he shovelled earth back into the hole, pausing now and then to tamp it down. When the cross was set, he knelt down to smooth the earth.

It was in this pose that Pam Ross first saw him. She watched him rise up, and in her eyes she saw a black shape that seemed to grow taller and taller as it rose from the grave. Then he turned, his head half-bowed as he glanced over his shoulder at her, the brim of his hat covering his eyes.

'I-I'm sorry,' she stammered. 'I didn't mean to disturb you.'

'You didn't,' he informed her. 'Just putting in a proper marker.'

'That's nice,' Pam smiled, sadly. 'Calvin deserved better than what the town gave him.' She stepped forward, eagerly, to see the new marker. Then gasped as she read the inscription.

'You've got it wrong,' she tried to explain, her voice tinged with panic. 'His name wasn't Calvin Nicholls Death.'

'Shows why he never used his last name,' the man in black said, gravely. 'He never did take to the way people pronounced it. It's De'Ath. Not Death.'

'You knew him, then?' she asked, still looking at the name carved along the crossbar of the cross.

'He was my brother,' the man in black informed her.

She smiled up at him. 'You must be Asa. He talked a lot about you.'

A ghost of a smile passed over his lips. It was there and then it was gone.

'You could say that,' he told her. 'Cal thought he was being kind. You see our pa had a sense of humour. He thought it was a laugh the way folks corrupted his name, so he named me after the Angel of Death—Asrael. Cal gentled it down some.' He paused to look down at her, an icy reserve cloaking him again to shut out the past. 'You came here with a purpose. Best I don't keep you.'

Pam stood there a little uncertain at

his sudden change of attitude, then pulled herself together, determined not to be put off by this strange, pale-faced man.

'It's an old habit,' she mentioned. 'Calvin and I used to talk to each other over dinner. We discussed things—' she faltered, as she gestured towards the grave. 'A habit I can't break, even though he's gone.'

'Leave you to it,' Asrael De'Ath murmured, turning his back on her to crouch down and begin the task of wrapping the shovel in the canvas.

'Do you have somewhere to stay?' she asked, watching his every move.

'No,' came the response.

'You could have Calvin's room,' Pam offered. 'I haven't been able to bring myself to clear it out. Let alone rent it out.'

He stood up, the canvas-wrapped bundle under his right arm.

'Obliged,' came the terse agreement.

She began to walk alongside him, aware

that his posture dictated that he did not require company. Yet she felt compelled to accompany him even if it was just to show him where her guest-house was.

'You got nothing to talk about?' he demanded. 'Or have you come to terms that you're only talking to the air?'

'Calvin understands.' A statement of which she was certain. 'He'd want me to take care of you.'

The man in black nodded. 'Even as a kid, Cal was like that. Always put others first. Pa called him soft.'

'Not like you.' She made it a statement.

His eyes shifted, fractionally, so that he could see her hard-set face.

'Not like me,' he agreed. 'Got no time for people. The one good thing about a corpse is that it don't keep talking back at you.'

'Demands your time, though,' she chuckled.

'Yeah,' he agreed and, again, a ghost of a smile flickered on his lips.

Pam guided him towards a flight of three steps that led up to the porch of her boarding-house. The man in black opened the door and stood back so that she could enter into the long hall. Flanked to one side was a flight of stairs, while to the other were two doors, the first of which opened on to her sitting-room, while the other gave access to the guests' dining-room. Pam did not lead him through either of these doors but through one set under the stairs. This opened on to a spacious, stone-flagged kitchen. To one side was the cooking range, a sink below a window with cupboards against another wall. In the centre was a well-scrubbed cooks' table with two chairs on one side. Another table was set below a hatch that served the dining-room.

'There's a hook behind the door,' she mentioned. 'That is if you want to hang your hat and coat.' She pointed at the range. 'I've got a stew warming if you're hungry.'

'Obliged,' he said, putting his burden down behind the door before removing his hat and coat and hanging them where indicated.

He rolled up the sleeves of his black shirt to just below the elbow to reveal strong forearms marked with ugly scar tissue that disappeared into his black gloves that he chose not to remove.

He saw Pam looking at them.

'Played with fire once,' he explained, as he sat down at the table. 'Tried my hand at blacksmithing when I was a boy—now I own the forge.'

'Is that what you do?' Pam asked, busying herself ladling hot stew on to a plate. 'Blacksmith?'

'That and some carpentry,' Death told her. 'Now I own my pa's business as well.'

'What did he do?' Pam enquired, bringing the plate over and setting it before him. 'Calvin never did say.'

'Undertaker,' came the sharp reply.

'Another joke?' Pam half-laughed as she went to the dresser to fetch him a fork and spoon.

'Could say that,' he conceded, watching her bring over a loaf of crusty bread from which she carved a generous slice. 'He was a qualified mortician. Taught me everything I know, so as I could carry on the family tradition.' He paused long enough to eat a spoonful of food. 'Calvin was never interested. Had other ideas. Plenty of ideas that he did nothing with.'

He felt as though he had talked too much. Once more he shrouded himself in the cold cloak and concentrated on eating his meal. Besides, the cosy conversation brought back vivid memories. It seemed as though the only time that father and son had talked had been over meals. Then he looked at the woman who was busy cleaning up the supper plates. He was providing a need for her by filling the void that his brother had left, which explained why she had not hung around the graveyard once she had discovered his identity.

'Calvin was a good lawman,' Pam mentioned, anxious to break the sudden silence. 'I liked him a lot, but—' Her voice trailed away as she lost herself in a brief memory. Then she caught herself. 'He seemed to keep me at a distance at times.'

Death nodded, understandingly. 'His way. Could never trust himself with women.'

Pam wiped her hands dry on a towel. 'In all the time I've known Calvin, I never thought about him being like that.'

'Guess you don't see things right,' Death shrugged. 'Not when you're up too close.'

Pam came over and sat beside him. 'Like you. I can't make you out. One minute your cold and distant—the next, well, you're like you are now.'

'Like I said,' he pointed out. 'I don't like people. Never hurts to talk, though, once in a while. Most of the time, they just leave me to get on with what I'm doing. That's the way I like it.'

'I'll leave you alone, then,' Pam shrugged, starting to rise.

'Rather you talked,' Death invited, pausing only to give her time to sit back down. 'Why don't you tell me how my brother came to die?'

It took her almost an hour to recount the events that led to the death of Calvin Nicholls. Not because it took that amount of time to tell, but because of the detail that the man in black sought out. He drained her of everything from names to descriptions, until he had a full visual description.

'So what is the law doing about my brother's murder?' he asked, as Pam poured him yet another cup of coffee, a chore she had carried out every fifteen minutes.

'Nothing,' she replied, shortly. 'Royce is the town marshal. Phelan is still a deputy. So is a man called Byrd. As far as they and Tunbridge are concerned, the case is closed.'

The man in black was silent for a moment while he sipped at the coffee. 'Then I'll open it again,' he decided, as he put the empty cup on the table.

'They are real trouble, Asa,' she warned, worriedly. 'They live, sleep and eat over at the law office. Anyone who gets too nosy—well, they just drop the subject. The town has just got to live with Calvin's death and they're prepared to let Tunbridge's men walk all over them.'

'That's other folks' problem,' Death stated, standing up. 'Not mine. My brother's dead and his killers are walking free. Do you really expect me to accept that?'

Pam looked up at his grim features and shook her head. 'No, Asa. I don't. I want them to pay for what they did. If I could use a gun—'

Death laid a hand on her shoulder and squeezed gently. 'Calvin wouldn't've wanted you to. With me, it's different. Calvin knew me too well; he'd expect me to bring a family problem to a conclusion.'

He went to the door and removed his hat and coat which he put on, his eyes fixed on the woman's back as he did so. Then he returned to her side and, once more, laid a reassuring hand on her shoulder.

'I'll be back,' he promised, before leaving her alone.

No one in his life had touched him the way Pam Ross had. He was used to getting on with his life without having to bother about other people's attitudes or feelings. The only time he made an exception was when people were buried, but even then his attitude was of one going through the motions because it went with the job.

One of the last things his father had told him was that one day he would meet someone who would break through that self-made barrier. 'Whatcha goin' to do, then?' his father had asked. To which Death had no answer. Now the question had risen its ugly head once more.

Another point he found difficult to understand was how a man who could not cope with women had laid all this trust in one. Calvin had and his brother could grasp the reason why. Pam Ross made no demands nor did she expect any to be made.

It was still with thoughts of the woman that Death entered the livery stable, but by the time he had passed through the doors he had put her from his mind. Once more that shadowy cloak shrouded his emotions, and his eyes narrowed as they adjusted to the dimly lit interior.

He walked quickly to the stall and rummaged in the hay until he located the saddle-bags he had hidden there. After unfastening a flap, he withdrew a plain, black double-rigged gunbelt, he checked each revolver in turn and practised a few draws. Satisfied, he walked out of the stall and stood in the middle of the stable.

Only when he felt that the time was right

to move did he leave the livery to walk down the main street at a cold, funereal pace. He paused at the door to the law office, composed himself and walked in.

In a quick glance he saw the lawman sitting behind his desk smoking a cheroot and blowing smoke rings at the ceiling, a dark-skinned man lounging on a cot in one of the cells and a young deputy sitting on another chair fiddling with his nails. His mind matched descriptions to the names of three men who were finding their company boring.

'Do something for you?' Royce asked, lazily.

Death just stood there, his arm moving enough to draw the overcoat away from the right-hand Colt.

He raised his head, enough so that the lawman could see his eyes. Royce's nose twitched as his forehead creased into a frown. It was as though he was staring into the eyes of someone he knew. Then is seemed to click. But the name was that of a man who was dead.

'I said,' Royce snarled, 'do something for you?'

Death moved fast, the gun seeming to leap from holster to fist to flame bullets in three directions as Death spun around to cover all three men.

'Just die,' Death suggested as the first bullet found its mark in Royce's chest.

The lawman went down hard, his dead weight crushing the wooden chair as both collapsed. Byrd was tossed on to his back to lie on the cot as though he had fallen asleep, which left Phelan gasping and shaken as he watched these events unfurl. Then he, too, was spinning and screaming as a bullet shattered his right shoulder. He crashed to the floor, fighting pain as his left hand groped for his gun which was trapped between his right thigh and the floor. Time was against him; a hand grabbed his left arm and hauled him to his feet. The gun was taken from its holster and tossed aside.

'Tunbridge,' Death said, harshly. 'I want him.'

'He—he's out of town,' Phelan sobbed through his pain, his left hand trying to staunch the flow of blood from his shattered shoulder.

Death reeled off the list of names but Phelan was unable to guess their whereabouts.

'You know,' Death insisted, 'and you are going to tell me.'

'The order was for them to scatter,' Phelan cried out. 'But to meet up again in Oakridge. That'd be about four of five days from now, I guess. Look,' his voice took on a pleading tone, 'you can find Lance at the Golden Slipper there. Lives with some whore. Why don't you go see him?'

Death nodded, digesting this information. Then looked at the cringing, pain-racked youth.

'Good of you to tell me so much,' Death said, softly.

'They sure as hell ain't worth dying for,'

Phelan sneered with a show of bravado. 'You finished now?'

Death nodded, drew his gun and fired one shot that hit Phelan between the eyes.

'Yeah,' he murmured. 'I'm finished with you.'

Death stepped out of the law office, aware of the shadows that lurked within the shadows. The audience was out to see the show but none of them were about to present an immediate threat to him. So he strode up the street to the livery.

The liveryman was standing by the door, the shot-gun slanted across his chest.

'Commotion down the street,' he mentioned, not attempting to block Death's route.

'Some,' Death acknowledged, striding towards the stall.

'It wouldn't have happened if Calvin was still alive,' the liveryman said bitterly, following behind the man in black.

'Where were you when they gunned

him down?' Death asked, retrieving his belongings.

'Trussed up like a Thanksgiving turkey in that end stall,' the liveryman growled. 'With Mel Johnson standing guard over me while the others did their dirty business.'

'That right?' Death grimaced, tossing the saddle-bags over his left shoulder and gripping a Sharps .50 buffalo gun in his left hand. 'Three of them found out what it's like to be on the receiving end.'

The liverymen started to laugh. 'Pleased to hear it.' He looked at the night beyond the open doors, then back again at the man in black who was no longer there. 'Best thing that's happened around here,' he said, anyway.

Death slipped, unobtrusively, back into the boarding-house but not before noting that most of the town seemed to be gathered outside the law office. Even had he used the main street to return, instead of the back alleys, he was certain that at least one person would have spotted him and drawn the attention of the crowd.

Pam Ross was still sitting in the kitchen, when he came in to drop his belongings alongside the canvas-wrapped shovel. Then he hung his coat and hat on a peg.

'I didn't think you would come back,' she mentioned, trying to sound matter of fact, not letting her emotions show through.

Although she failed in this, Death did not attempt to disillusion her. He went to the stove and poured himself a cup of coffee which he drank with his back to her.

'I'll be gone in the morning,' he stated.

'I don't think bad of you,' Pam confessed, standing up to cross the room to stand at his side. 'It had to be done. The town knows what happened after they shot Sam Vennor. Tunbridge would've found a way to get them off.' She sighed. 'You know, right now, I want to be shot of this town. Just sell up and move away. Everybody wants something for nothing. They—'

Death turned to silence her by touching her lips with one black leather-clad finger.

'I know how you feel,' he told her, softly. 'People are the same no matter where you go. Towns grow and towns die. Never been any different. But it is people who destroy the good things in life, to line their own pockets.'

Pam licked her lips. 'I'm coming with you, tomorrow. I want to see Calvin's killers die.'

Death shook his head. 'Rest assured, they will die. Be content with that.'

Pam wanted to argue, but when she saw the ice in his eyes, she let the words of protest die. He was right, she should be content. At the same time she did not want him to put his life as risk to gain his own vengeance. Any attempt, she knew, to argue the point would have been futile.

He laid his hands on her shoulders. 'How about showing me to my room?' he suggested.

Pulling herself together, Pam suggested

that he follow her to the top floor where a spacious attic room was situated, with a single bed, dresser, wardrobe and bureau ranged around the walls. A window was set in the slope of roof and Death could imagine Calvin lying on the bed staring up at the stars.

When he was alone, he opened doors and drawers to find nothing more than the few clothes that his brother had possessed. Seven or so books were balanced on top of the roll-top bureau; the titles ranging from a history of the Civil War to a cheap dime novel. On seeing these Death smiled for his memory of Calvin was one of a great reader who let his imagination get the better of him.

He tried to open the roll-top, but found it locked. Unable to find the key and unwilling to disturb Pam, he forced it open to find a half-written letter and a lacquered box. This he opened to find eleven letters, all addressed to Calvin care of the telegraph office, all of them from

Death himself and kept like a special treasure.

He picked up the half-written letter and lay on the bed to read it by the flickering candlelight. After the usual show of affection for his brother, the letter began to tell him about the problems that were building up in town, the bribery and corruption that was rife and a plea for help and advice on what to do.

All of which served to fuel the anger that burned in Death's soul.

He rolled from the bed, suddenly finding the room too claustrophobic. He had to get out and go anywhere knowing that he could not say the things that needed to be said.

Donning his hat and coat, Death went out into the night. He stood on the porch and savoured the coolness of the night air. The night was his time, a shadow who could drift by unseen; alone with his thoughts that no one could invade with unasked for advice or opinions.

He went to the cemetery and crouched by his brother's grave.

'You damn stupid fool,' he said to the earth. 'This was no way to prove that you were a man. So you made a mess of your life and I know Pa never allowed you to live it down. But to die the way you did—no man deserves that kind of punishment.' Despite the sorrow, his tone was colder than the grave. 'Well, Calvin, at least three souls rest in peace. The rest will follow, that's a promise, Brother.'

He stood up, but his eyes were fixed on the earth, as though he could see Calvin's corpse. Could see into the dead eyes and read the dead man's last thoughts.

Then he turned away and walked, slowly, back to the boarding-house, back to his room. There he lay, fully clothed, on the bed and fell into a dreamless sleep.

The morning light streamed through the uncurtained window set in the slope of the roof. Death's eyes snapped open and he sat up, before swinging his legs over the bed so that he could sit on the edge.

His mind came instantly alert. The course of the day mapped out. Then he thought about Pam, his mouth turning down, grimly, and his eyes narrowing. It was one thing to move on: another to just leave her. There had never been a woman like her in his life before. His pa had despaired of both his sons; one because he could not have a relationship with a woman, and the other who could not hold a woman's attention long enough. Death had always been shy with women and being the undertaker's boy did not help. There were the jokes and, in any case, there had to be something weird about a man who worked with corpses.

The only thing that had kept Pam interested in him was the fact that Calvin linked them. Come the clear light of morning, the closeness between them would be nothing.

It was in that frame of mind that he went down to breakfast, heading straight for the dining-room where two drummers glanced at him. After satisfying their curiosity they resumed their breakfast.

Death sat in a dark corner, out of everyone's way.

Pam breezed in, to take a glance around to see if there was a table to clear, then saw Death waiting for her to serve him.

'Asa,' she greeted, coming over to stand by him. 'Sleep well?'

'Like the dead,' he growled.

Pam laughed. 'Come into the kitchen,' she invited. 'You'll be more comfortable.'

He followed her and sat down, waiting as she cooked bacon, eggs and fried bread, all of which she served him with a smile.

'I thought you might be moving on today,' she stated. 'I've made up some beef sandwiches. I've also made some sourdough bread. Anything else I can get you?'

'You've done too much, already,' he assured her. 'How much do I owe you?'

'Nothing,' she shrugged. 'I just want to help. That's all.'

'All?' he queried, sure there was a catch or that she just wanted to be rid of him now.

Pam blushed and looked down at her hands.

'Just promise me one thing, Asa,' she murmured, softly. 'Just promise me that when it's all over, you'll come back safe.'

A ghost of a smile passed over his lips. 'I'll be back.'

SEVEN

Two men, then, with their thoughts as Friday 13th began to fade away with the approach of the midnight hour.

Willard Dull tried to clear his mind of recent events and turn back to the book that he had been reading. Concentration refused to come as his memory was plagued by the pale face of the man in black. A familiar face, yet unfamiliar. Certain that their paths had not crossed recently, he tried to delve back to other times but a name would not come to the surface. He could not dismiss the matter as a case of mistaken identity, as he prided himself on never forgetting a face.

While Dull sought an identity, Death paced the room above. He had not wanted to think about Pam Ross—not when he had more pressing things to attend to.

To divert his mind, he checked his two guns once more, then holstered them beneath the heavy looking overcoat. Then he tightened the black leather gloves over his hands, to ensure that his fingers were free of snags. It was time to go.

As he descended the stairs, his narrow eyes watched as Dull looked up. For a moment, panic flooded the government man's eyes; then quickly he masked it, appearing uninterested as he dropped his eyes back to the printed page.

Death paused. Standing stock still and silent, he stared down at the man who was pretending to read. When Dull could stand it no longer, he looked up but Death had passed by. Dull swivelled his head, so that he could see out of the window. Death was halfway across the street, walking at a funereal pace until he stopped outside the batwing doors of the saloon opposite.

Death surveyed the interior. A bar ran

down the length of the room to his left. Tables and chairs, most of which were empty now due to the lateness of the hour, filled most of the middle section, from which a staircase rose to rooms above. The right-hand side of the saloon was set aside for gambling; whether it be cards, craps or the wheel of fortune. Two card tables were still active and so was the craps table where three men were rattling hard to clear a fourth of his money. Three tired and bored saloon girls ambled about hoping that someone would take up an offer that, sober, they would have refused.

Into this stepped Death. He ambled over to the bar, where the solitary barman was busy cleaning glasses. The barman was square headed and heavily built, his blue and white striped shirt just about fitting him. Pouched eyes watched the man in black approach, and his thin lips grimaced with a promise of refusal.

'Kinda late, mister,' he said, deciding

that he would serve one drink and that would be the stranger's limit. 'Get you somethin'?'

'Hepburn Lance,' Death stated.

'Not at this time of night, mister.' The barman was firm. 'You got business with him, you try again come daylight.' He glared at the silent man, waiting for a response and when none came asked, 'Now do you want a drink or not?'

The man in black moved with deceptive speed as his left arm shot out to grab the startled barman around his thick neck. Death yanked hard and the barman yelped with pain as his ribs cracked against the solid wood of the edge of the bar. Then Death shoved him back, his hand still locked on the barman's neck. This as the barman's hands came up to clutch at his damaged midsection. Death pulled him forward again with a force that broke two fingers as one of the barman's hands slammed into the counter.

'You bas—' the barman roared through

tears of pain, before the grip tightened shutting off the oath.

'Hepburn Lance,' Death demanded, his voice full of cold menace.

'I can't,' the barman protested. 'It's more'n my job's worth.'

'Better to lose your job, than to lose your life,' Death growled.

The barman's eyes glanced towards the stairs, then towards the craps table where a man in a well-worn grey suit had edged away from the other players.

'Room three,' the bar man gasped.

'You better be right,' Death warned. 'You don't want me to come back for you.'

'I ain't lying, mister,' the barman promised, desperate to be free from Death's grasp.

'One more thing,' Death suggested, 'put whatever it is you keep under the bar—on it.'

The barman groped about, his eyes fixed on those of the man who held him. He produced a shot-gun and laid it gently on the bar top.

Death let go his grip and dropped his hand to the weapon. He flipped it open and shucked the shells before skidding the shot-gun along the bartop until it fell to the floor at the other end. By then the barman had been flung back against the rack of glasses behind him, some toppling to crack him about the head and body as he sagged to a glass-littered floor.

'Just stay there,' the man in black warned.

A redheaded craps player, acting on a signal from the grey-suited man began to edge towards the batwing doors. There he paused waiting to see what happened next.

The man in black stepped towards the stairs, then turned his head slightly, and looked straight at the grey-clad man.

'It's not your time yet,' he warned, watching as grey suit's hand paused on its slow journey to the butt of a Peacemaker holstered across his middle.

Slowly, he began his ascent of the stairs, all the while his senses alerted to the actions of those men who posed a threat behind him.

The barman stayed where he was, while the man in the grey suit could do nothing more than let his hand fall away from the gun butt, as he exchanged glances with and shrugged at the redhead by the door. The third of the craps players who had been fleecing a brown-suited drummer decided that it was time to cut and run. He was through the batwings before the redhead could stop him.

'What do we do?' the redhead asked.

'Nothing,' grey suit responded. 'Think about it Mel. With old Hep outa the way I get to keep all the profits.'

Mel Johnson gave the other a surprised look. 'So much for loyalty.'

'You want to tackle that fella?' the other asked.

Mel Johnson shook his head and went back to his post.

The man in black reached the top of the stairs where he stopped to stand motionless while he listened. From beyond the door marked with a brass number 3 he could hear movement and the creak of bedsprings followed by a derogatory laugh that came from a female throat.

'What's with you, Hep?' The woman's voice was coarse and spiteful. 'You lost it or somethin'?'

'It's been a long time, hon,' a male voice whined.

'Too old more like,' the woman rasped.

'Makes him ready for the grave, lady,' the man in black muttered as he lifted his right leg high and thrust it at the door.

It splintered under the force administered to it, and slammed free from one hinge as it crashed into the wall. Death stood in the gaping doorway, his shadow cast on to the bed where a woman was sitting up and a man was halfway out.

The woman screamed, her hands scrabbling at the bedclothes as she attempted to cover her nakedness, while Lance pulled them away in an attempt to do the same.

'What the hell is this?' Lance yelled, his eyes darting to where his gun was encased in a holster hanging from the brass bedhead—out of reach.

'Judgement day,' Death announced as he drew the right-hand Colt from beneath his overcoat and fired two shots.

Both bullets took Lance in the centre of his scrawny chest, the force of which flung him backwards into a dresser. The corpse bounced forwards to land back on the bed from where it slid down to the floor. Clawed hands dragged the covers with him, which had the screaming woman chasing after them.

'I wouldn't bother, lady,' Death snorted. 'I can see you had nothing to hide.'

He turned away and left the room to stand at the top of the stairs. Looking down he saw the grey-suited man waiting at the bottom. This time he had the Peacemaker in his hand and he was aiming it upwards.

'You know who I am?' he demanded. 'I'm Cole Colby.'

Death did not hesitate. He fired three shots and stood there unemotionally as Colby was spun around, trying to hold on to life as he doubled over and took two steps towards the bar before crashing face down.

'At least I know what to put on the tombstone,' the man in black stated as he came down the stairs.

Above and behind him, the woman's screams had changed to sobs interspersed with invective levelled at both the dead man and his killer. At least the woman did not pose a threat to him, not like the stunned redhead who was grasping one of the batwing doors. It was a straight choice of whether he was going to run or draw. Death waited, giving the redhead a chance to make a decision.

Mel Johnson ran.

Death waited, watching the swinging batwings until they had stopped.

'Do—do you mind if I go?' This from the nervous drummer who was crouched behind the craps table. 'I've nothing to do with all this.'

Death emptied his gun of spent cartridges and replaced them with fresh bullets.

'Do what you like,' Death suggested. 'I haven't come for you.' Then he looked at the terrified drummer. 'Suggest you have a whiskey before you go. Settles the nerves.'

'I'll—I'll take you up on that,' the drummer stammered coming out from behind his shelter.

'Just made a suggestion,' Death advised. 'Didn't offer to buy you one.'

'On the house,' the barman offered, grateful that he could get back to his feet. Then to the man in black, 'Can I get you something?'

Death ignored the question, instead asked, 'The redhead?'

The barman gave the name.

'Hope he realizes that he's lucky to be alive,' Death stated, referring to the fact that he was not after Mel for that man had not been involved in the killing of his brother.

'Poured you a drink,' the barman mentioned, as Death began to walk towards the doors.

'Don't drink fella,' Death remarked as he exited from the saloon to return to the hotel.

Willard Dull was beside himself with curiosity. He had wanted to cross the road to see for himself what had happened and knew that it was bad. This conclusion he had come to the moment the first shots were fired and later confirmed when Mel Johnson had come tearing out to run full-pelt up town.

He was tempted to ask the night clerk, Tom Quimby, to go and see what had happened but the aged, crippled ex-cowpuncher was nowhere to be seen.

Then Death entered. He did not look at Dull but walked right by him and headed for the stairs. Halfway up, he paused but did not look back.

'You know what curiosity did?' he mentioned. 'It got someone killed. Hate for you to go before your time, Dull.'

Dull gaped as he watched the black apparition fade up the stairs. A cold shudder ran through him as he realized that Death had spoken his name. It made him wonder, once again, about the familiar face of a man whom he was sure he had never met. But they must have done, Dull tried to reason, for how else could he have known his name?

At the Cattleman's Hotel further up the street, Major Samuel Tunbridge was not happy at having his poker game disturbed. He was $2000 ahead and holding a full house with close to $5000 in the pot.

The other four men around the table had already thrown in their hands apart from the hotel owner, Gus McLintock, who was rubbing his sweat-tacky, bald, freckled head as he tried to work out whether Tunbridge was bluffing or holding a hand that would damage the hotelier financially.

'Right,' McLintock decided. 'Five hundred plus another five.'

'You should quit while you are ahead,' Tunbridge suggested. 'One day you are going to gamble that once too many and I will end up owning this place.'

'You already got a half-share,' Wes Dooley, a florid-looking Texan rancher laughed. 'Most of it out of your gambling debts, Gus.'

'One day I'll get it all back,' Gus promised without conviction.

'Not with your luck,' Tunbridge advised, leaning forward to add a wad of notes to the growing pile. 'Five plus a thousand.'

McLintock looked at the small pile of notes in front of him, short fingers on a podgy hand spreading them out. He sighed as he added the denominations together. It was decision time. He could brave it out and maybe find himself having to make out an IOU which would have to be repaid with a share of his hotel, or he could just fold and hold on to what he had. He had built up the business by himself and already he had lost half of it; anymore and it would be Tunbridge who would make all the decisions.

Reluctantly, he folded the cards together and threw them face down on the table.

'I quit,' he said, standing up and pulling his jacket tighter around him, a gesture of defiance. 'I guess my card-playing days are over.'

Tunbridge's eyes narrowed. 'You sound like a drunk taking the pledge. It never lasts.'

'I will,' Gus fired back. 'I get to keep what I built up.' He stabbed an angry finger at Tunbridge. 'All you get is a share of the profits.'

Tunbridge just smiled. 'You know me, Gus. If I want something I usually get it.'

'Not this hotel,' Gus snapped back, picking up his money and pocketing it.

Sensing the tension between the two men, the other card players picked up their cash and left.

'I'm sorry you feel that way, Gus,' Tunbridge stated with mock sincerity. 'We could both become wealthy men. You know that whatever I have an interest in, there is always a healthy profit.'

'I'm not listening,' Gus retorted. 'Nothing you do is on the level—or so I hear. I'm not stupid.'

Tunbridge smiled maliciously. 'Except when it comes to cards.'

'I'm not standing for this, Tunbridge,' Gus roared. 'Make sure you check out tomorrow.'

Without awaiting any more argument, Gus McLintock stormed out of the small gaming-room. As he did so, Tunbridge leaned forward and counted out $500 and set them aside.

'Thank you, Jerome,' he said.

From the shadows came a tall Negro attired in a black jacket and pants, the white of his shirt a stark contrast to the rest of his colouring. He had stood there unobtrusively all evening, emerging only to replenish the drinks of the card players from crystal decanters ranged on a trolley.

And because Jerome was out of sight, it was construed that he was out of mind also, which was why Tunbridge paid him generously to signal a code that would identify the cards in McLintock's hand.

'Yo' almos' pulled it off,' Jerome commiserated. 'Yo sho' one good boss, Major Tunbridge, suh.'

Tunbridge smiled up at the black giant. 'I will still pull it off, Jerome I am not just good at cards: you could say that no matter what I do I always keep a poker face.'

Jerome let loose a deep-throated guffaw.

'That sho' was a good one.'

'I'll be back in a few days, Jerome,' Tunbridge mentioned, sliding back his chair and standing up. 'I may well have a new job for you. Good money too.'

'I'll be here,' Jerome promised as he began to clear away the used glasses.

Once outside of the room, Tunbridge's manner changed. He signalled, angrily, at Mel Johnson who was sitting nervously, in the foyer. Mel stood up and followed Tunbridge up to the major's second floor-room.

'Just what do you think you mean?' Tunbridge rounded on him, as Johnson closed the door. 'Barging into a serious game of poker like that and demanding to talk to me.'

Mel shifted, anxiously, from one foot to the other. On the one hand angry at being talked down to in such a way, while on the other too scared of the major to say what he felt.

'Colby and Lance are dead,' Mel blurted

out. 'Fella just walked in. Got Lance in bed. Then took care of Colby.'

The major digested this information then demanded, 'Where were you? Why did you not back up Lance and Colby.'

'Colby told me to keep out of it,' Mel admitted. 'All Colby could see was that he would have the saloon if Lance was dead.'

'He always was greedy,' Tunbridge snorted. 'Spent as fast as he got it. Still, why did you not back up Colby?'

'Someone had to let you know what had happened,' Mel said, defensively. ''Sides you wouldn't've wanted to tackle that fella. I tell you, Major, he was black as death and twice as fast as any I've seen. I'd've stood no chance and my brothers would've come looking for him—and then there'd be none of us left.'

The panted-out explanation made sense to Tunbridge who had calmed down somewhat, compared to the way he had felt when he had summoned Mel to the room.

'Colby was always too greedy for his own good,' Tunbridge acknowledged. 'The thing to do right now, though, is to close ranks. I want you to round up the rest of the men—I do not care where they are or what they are doing—just find them and get them down to the abattoir. They will have to stay the night there until I find out what is going on.'

Mel Johnson acknowledged the order before backing, as fast as he could, out of the room.

After Mel had gone, Tunbridge reached into the inside pocket of his jacket and withdrew a yellowish slip of paper which he unfolded and read with growing concern. Deep in thought, he dropped the paper on to the bed and paced the room. Five of his men were now dead; another killing would put all his planning in jeopardy. At least, he assumed, the others would have a chance once they were in a place of safety.

He crossed the room, knocked on the

connecting door and waited until Amos Biggelow opened it. Tunbridge told him what had happened and then showed him the telegraph. The line of Biggelow's turned-down mouth grew deeper and his lower lip protruded as he digested the information.

'Dull?' he queried.

'Not his way,' Tunbridge stated, knowledgeably yet cautious.

'Then he's got someone to do the killin's for him,' Biggelow proposed, handing back the telegraph slip. 'Want me to go and find out?'

'We have to find Dull, first,' Tunbridge pointed out, almost spitting the words out.

'Bates Hotel,' Biggelow shrugged, to hide his smugness at knowing something that the major did not.

Tunbridge glared at him. 'How long have you known this?'

'Tonight,' Biggelow told him. 'Saw him standing outside just before the storm hit.

You was busy playing cards, so I kept quiet 'til you was ready.'

Tunbridge hated to make concessions, especially when Biggelow had followed orders. Had it not been for the news that he had received, Tunbridge would have been content to wait until morning to know that Dull was around. Now though, Dull's appearance coinciding with the death of two men took on a more sinister appearance.

Tunbridge smiled. 'I think I will call on Dull, personally, in the morning. Just watch my back, Amos, keep it well covered.'

'Count on it,' Biggelow promised.

The drummer, his nerves calmer now that he had imbibed three free whiskeys, ambled over to the Bates Hotel. He was unaware that he was being watched until he crossed the threshold and became aware of Dull sitting on the *chaise-longue*.

'You look like a man with a lot on his mind,' the drummer observed, leaning over the desk to flip his room key from the keyboard.

'Were you in the saloon when the shootings took place?' Dull asked, officiously.

The drummer turned and leaned on the counter, his free hand jiggling the key up and down.

'Was I there?' the drummer asked, incredulous that he should be asked that question. 'You know I've only just started to cover this area. Two days ago I was in a place called Summerhill when someone just strolls into the law office in the middle of the night and wipes the whole lot out. Then tonight, two more killings. You know what my boss said? "The West isn't that bad anymore".'

'Is that right?' Dull growled, uninterested in what the drummer's boss had or had not said.

What concerned him was the report at what had occurred at Summerhill. Already he was becoming alarmed and knew that he had to find a way to get this Death character out of the case. For he was certain that Death had disposed of those men at Summerhill.

'I don't suppose you saw who did the killings?' Dull wondered. 'The ones up at Summerhill.'

The drummer shook his head. 'No one saw a thing. There were people around but no one saw anyone go into the law office or come out again.'

Dull nodded. 'Obliged for your time.'

'Think nothing of it,' the drummer shrugged. 'It's all an eye-opener to me you know. Nothing like the dime novels I read back East.'

'Nothing ever is,' Dull agreed, distractedly for the news disturbed him.

If what the drummer had said was true and half of Tunbridge's men had been eliminated, then weeks of careful planning were about to fall apart. Death had to be stopped before there was any more killing. If talking to the man in black achieved nothing, then he could always work in alliance with Tunbridge. What his men had done to Nicholls, they could do to Death. At least Dull would emerge from the whole mess with his hands clean.

'Well, good night,' the drummer called out, realizing that Dull had lost interest in their conversation.

'Yes, good night,' Dull acknowledged, then asked by way of a friendly gesture, 'I take it you will be leaving in the morning?'

'Slickett's Hill,' the drummer mentioned. 'I understand that there is a small store there.'

'By the station,' Dull pointed out. 'That's all there is there. A station and a store. You should have a peaceful time there.'

'I hope so.' The drummer gave a half chuckle.

'So do I,' Dull responded, hopefully.

Dull stood up and laid his book down on the *chaise longue.* For a moment he stared out of the window, his face grim. Then, decisively, he left the hotel, to stride, purposefully, up to the telegraph office. It was closed and in darkness but Dull knew that the operator slept close to his equipment. So Dull hammered on the door until he was rewarded by a glimmer of light that indicated that a lamp had been lit. Within a few seconds he heard the sound of bolts being drawn and a key turn in the lock. The door opened a crack.

'What the hell you want?' the operator demanded grumpily, leaden eyes trying to stay open long enough to recognize the late-night visitor.

'To send an urgent telegraph,' Dull informed him, as he shoved against the door.

The tired operator was unable to offer any resistance, so he stepped back to allow Dull to enter. Once inside, Dull, shut the door. He located the telegraph key and sat down in front of it.

'Leave it alone,' the operator said,

wearily. 'I'll send your message. We operators recognize each other's touch, you see.'

Dull stood up to allow the operator to sit down. He pulled a pad towards him, then licked the point of a pencil, before glancing up at Dull.

'Right mister,' the operator snapped. 'What's the message?'

Dull told him.

The operator shoved the pad away. 'No point in sending that. Already had that information come through.' He reached for a box and sorted through his copies of messages received. 'Here we are.' He thrust the message form at Dull. 'Royce. Byrd. Phelan. They got killed up at Summerhill. Message came through for Major Tunbridge.'

A cold chill swept through Dull. Tunbridge was in town and he did not know it. He had been waiting for his arrival, but the man had not been seen. Maybe, Dull mused, he was losing his touch.

'I did not know that Tunbridge was in town,' Dull admitted, fishing for information.

'Gave him the message myself,' the operator said, daring Dull to challenge him.

'I do not doubt you,' Dull said, hastily.

The clock behind him chimed midnight. Friday 13th had gone into history. Dull hoped that Saturday 14th would see a more favourable change in his fortunes. Somehow, he felt, things would get worse.

EIGHT

Out of habit, Death awoke at five in the morning. He lay, fully dressed, on the bed staring at the ceiling. Once he was awake he had to get up and do something for no matter how much he had tried in the past, he could not go back to sleep.

He rolled from the bed and approached the dresser, pouring cold water from a rose-patterned jug into a matching bowl. After splashing water over his face and washing his hands he dried himself on a rough towel which he tossed on to a nearby chair. He moved to the wardrobe and took his overcoat from a hanger and put it on. Then he removed his hat from the bedhead and, using both hands, set it on his head, all the while making sure that the brim was pulled down low over his face.

Locking the door behind him, the man in black descended the stairs to the deserted foyer. He stepped out of the hotel, to stand on the boardwalk, his eyes taking in the dark silence of the main street. To the east the sky showed the first glimmer of the coming dawn. Death chose to meet the new day.

His pace was slow and purposeful as he passed by the cheaper saloons, hotels and cathouses. Beyond lay the tanneries, the abattoirs and warehouses. A freight train, belching black smoke and spitting fire from its belly had been shunted onto a spur line. A man shouted, his voice splitting the night. A gate was opened which slammed against a fenced enclosure and there was a loud bellow as cattle were prodded out, their hooves tapping against a wooden board that led into a cattle truck. Further up a wagon was being backed against a caboose, and men closed in ready to unload crates for stacking inside.

A stench rose from the tanneries and the

abattoirs: a mixture of raw meat, blood and steaming fat, cattle and their droppings. The smell of death hung thickly, yet it did not make the man in black feel at home as others might suppose.

He stood in the shadows and watched the town come to life. Then with a sigh he turned away to walk between two abattoirs with the intention of drifting out into the fringes of the town to get a breath of fresh air only to stop and drift back into the shadows as three men emerged from one of the slaughterhouses.

While Death had been watching the train being loaded, Major Tunbridge had been talking to his men. He had informed them about the deaths of five of their number, letting them know that he felt that it was, by their actions, their fault.

'What in the world did you think you were doing?' he demanded, sitting authoritatively behind the desk in the office sited at the back of the slaughterhouse. 'First rustling cattle, then gunning down

Vennor. It seems to me that from one foolhardy moment—'

'Just you hold on there, Major,' Deke Tinsley spoke up, as he rested one cheek of his backside on the edge of the desk. 'You ain't layin' no blame on us. Guess we were a bit sick 'n' tired of doin' nothin'. The cattle just seemed like a good idea—at the time.'

Tunbridge's eyes narrowed, his lips thinning with anger. He was not used to being spoken to like this.

'If we are to survive,' he said, curtly, 'you must still take orders. Damn it, man, I am trying to keep the rest of you alive.'

'Appreciate your concern, Major,' Tinsley acknowledged. 'But the way I figure it, we got a right to do things our way—sometimes. Ain't none of us in the army now.' A comment which received grunts and nods of approval from the three Johnson brothers. 'Right now, the way I figure it, is that we should be concentratin' on the next job. Not goin' over things that are past.'

Tunbridge glared at Tinsley but when he saw that the other did not bear any animosity towards him, began visibly to relax.

'Fair enough,' Tunbridge conceded. 'To the matter in hand, then. I suggest that you proceed to Slickett's Hill immediately. Leave your horses there and board the train once you are sure that the army payroll has been loaded. There will be four carriages, a baggage car and a caboose. The caboose will be at the back of the train. It will have just the one way in from the baggage car, apart from the sliding doors on either side. Remember this train will also be carrying mail bags, so do not collect the wrong bags. I have ordered two crates which will be in the baggage car. Transfer the payroll to the crates.' Then he glanced at Mel Johnson. 'Mel will meet you at the linesman's shack, which is at the top of the incline between Oakridge and Summerhill. The train will be going slow enough for you to get off. Once you have left the train return to Oakridge and stay here until you hear from me. Any questions?'

The Johnsons shook their heads, while Tinsley just shrugged. The plan seemed simple enough to them and they would follow it through. Minor details, like getting into the caboose they would sort out for themselves.

Tunbridge stood up, as Biggelow opened the door for him. The Major hesitated, then beckoned Mel Johnson to follow him. The youngest of the three red-faired brothers followed Tunbridge out of the office.

The three men were silent as they walked up the street, none of them aware of the man in black who was now following them.

'Mel, I have a small job for you,' Tunbridge mentioned. 'I want you to get yourself noticed. Especially, by Dull.

With luck, by the time he misses you, you will be on your way to the lineshack.' He paused but did not give Mel Johnson time to protest. 'I have had fresh mounts purchased at the Murchison livery. All you have to do is collect them.'

'If I'm still alive,' Mel Johnson grumbled. 'Fine showin' meself off to Dull. But what about that man in black?'

'Leave that to me,' Tunbridge stated. 'I think Dull has something to do with that. I will have him call his killer off.'

'I hope so,' Johnson prayed.

The man in black allowed a faint smile to pass over his lips. Mel Johnson had nothing to fear from him, for the redhead was destined to lead him to the others. Satisfied, he ducked into a doorway and waited until the others had passed out of sight.

The sun was up by the time Death entered the hotel and made straight for the dining-room. Only three other guests had come down for breakfast so far, so Death had the pick of the tables. He sat at one that put a wall against his back, so that he could watch who came and went through the double glass doors that gave on to the dining-room.

Jason Bates came out of the kitchen door set midway up the room, he glanced around and spotted Death. Such was his surprise that he almost dropped the two plates of eggs, bacon and hash browns that he was carrying. Quickly, he threaded his way through the tables and laid the loaded plates in front of his customers. Then came rushing down to the man in black.

'This table's reserved,' he said politely, dry washing his hands.

'Nothing to say so,' the man in black pointed out.

'I don't do that,' Bates whined. 'It's knowledge around here that when the Hincks boys are in town—well, this is their table.'

'They buy it?' Death asked, coldly.

'I did, but—' Bates protested, nervously.

'Then they've no claim to it,' Death decided. 'They either wait 'till I've finished or they use another table. Simple as that.'

'Your funeral, mister,' Bates surrendered. 'Don't say I didn't warn you. Them Hincks boys get real mean.'

'Then I'll settle for a hearty breakfast,' the man in black murmured, the faintest shadow of a smile passing over his lips.

Bates just nodded and backed away turning towards the kitchen door as Willard Dull made his entrance. He paused just inside the doors as he spotted Death sitting in the dark corner of the room. Then his gaze drifted to the hesitant Bates who jerked his head, meaningfully, at the seated man.

'He's trouble,' Bates mentioned.

Dull nodded. 'Not for long, Jase.'

'I want him out before the Hincks boys come down,' Bates protested, hoping that there was something that Dull could do.

'Not my problem, Jase,' Dull pointed

out, kindly. 'I will talk to him, though. Not that I expect him to take any notice of me.'

'Anything you can do, Mister Dull.' Jason looked as though he was thankful. 'I sure appreciate it.'

Dull ambled over to Death's table as Bates scurried into the sanctuary of his kitchen.

'Mind if I join you?' Dull asked, pulling out a chair determined to sit down whether or not he was invited to do so.

Death did not bother to look up.

'You do what you think is right,' Death's voice was low.

Dull sat down and leaned forward to rest his elbows on the edge of the table.

'Last night,' Dull mentioned, 'you knew who I was.'

Death said nothing, just sat there waiting for the government man to say what he had to say.

Dull realized that he was not going to draw any information from the silent man, so decided to press on regardless.

'Five men are dead,' Dull stated. 'I needed those men alive to stand trial. Now, I suppose I am right in assuming, you are a bounty hunter. I am authorized to pay you five thousand dollars to ride away.' When he received no reaction to his offer, Dull continued, 'Five thousand dollars is twice the amount of the bounty you would receive.'

Death lifted his head, the wide brim just exposing his eyes; cold eyes that bored into those of Willard Dull.

'Dull'—the voice was as cold as his eyes—'I am not a bounty hunter. I am a collector of lives. Only when the last of those men I have come for are dead and buried will I go away.'

Dull shuddered, his windpipe jerking with fear as he listened to the finality in Death's tone.

'Go away, now, Death,' Dull said, not feeling so confident. 'I want those men.'

'Dull,' Death intoned, 'I know the depths

of your soul. I know how you bribed and ordered others to take bribes. How you exploited the weaknesses of others to achieve your own ends. You can't touch me, Dull. I came here with a purpose and I'll not go 'til I've done.'

Dull stood up, abruptly, the force tipping over his chair.

'Mister, you have trouble coming,' Dull warned. 'The last person who sat at this table ended up on Boot Hill. I promise you, I will be at your burying.' He began to walk away looking for another table to sit at; then turned around long enough to say, 'Damn you Death, I will see you in hell for this.'

Death lifted his head long enough to reply, 'Don't tempt fate, Dull.'

Dull ignored the command as he sat at a table by the window where he watched, sullenly, as Jason Bates came out of the kitchen shaking his head as he saw Death had not moved, before sidling up to the table to serve what he believed was going to be Death's last breakfast.

An uneasy air seemed to settle on the dining-room as some guests ate their breakfasts hastily, so as to be out of the way when trouble started. While Dull waited with the assurance that the Hinckses would put an end to his problems. Jason Bates hid, with trepidation, knowing that another death at his hotel would give it a reputation it did not deserve. He wondered if there was something that he could do or say that would prevent the Hinckses from coming down.

As he emerged from the kitchen he knew that nothing was going to prevent the inevitable for Shawn and Nathan Hincks were already entering the dining-room. Both men were tall, an inch or so over six feet; blond and muscular with identical looks that suggested that they were twins except that Shawn was two years older. Both had square, arrogant chins, piercing blue eyes and smiling, confident mouths. They looked like men who took nothing

181

and nobody seriously, except that the deceptive eyes could turn to steel in a blink of an eyelid.

Shawn wore a light grey suit with a white shirt and a black bootlace tie, while his brother was attired in brown cords and a yellow shirt, that showed off the muscular lines of his twenty-year-old body. Both wore tied-down gun belts, and the positions of their right hands suggested that they were always ready to use their Colts.

None of this impressed the man in black who was already half-way through his meal. Death glanced to his left, to watch Dull set aside his breakfast so that he could lean his weight on his elbows as he watched, with obvious anticipation, the Hincks boys approach the table.

'Bates,' Shawn Hincks roared. 'This fella's got our table. You tell him it was reserved?'

'He told me,' Death stated, evenly, cutting into the yolk of his egg and spearing a piece of bacon into it. 'Now I'll tell you. You either wait 'til I've finished or you go to another table.' Death paused to put food into his mouth. 'There is a third option.'

'Which is?' Shawn prompted, leaning forward, bracing himself to draw his gun.

Death ignored the question to put more food in his mouth which he chewed, steadily. The situation that he was in seemed to be going in one direction, for he was faced with a pair of bullies who were used to having their own way.

He spared a glance at Dull and knew that the government man would offer no assistance in a situation where the outcome could be to his advantage. Not that Death was that bothered by the threat imposed by the Hinckses.

'I think he's threatenin' us,' Nathan spoke out, his voice a touch girlish.

'Nobody threatens us,' Shawn snarled. 'No more talkin' fella. Move—or we move you.'

Death finished his mouthful and looked at his empty plate. Then at the mug of coffee that had gone cold. That could wait, he decided.

Neither man was expecting the speed with which the man in black rose to his feet. The table tilted over, hovered for a moment before crashing down, the edge slamming into the arch of Nathan's left foot. He overbalanced and fell to the floor, screaming shrilly as he clutched at his injured limb. Death ignored him, concentrating on the gun-drawing, half-bent-forward Shawn. Death's hand shot out grabbing the older Hincks by the front of his shirt, pulling him forward, as Death's left fist powered into his belly. Shawn screamed with pain, his grip on his gun loosened so that the half-drawn weapon fell to the floor. Death did not let up as his fist hammered time and again into Shawn's belly and ribs. Abruptly, Death pushed Shawn away, forcing him to trip over his brother and lie curled up on the dining-room carpet gasping for air.

'There's only one more option to you,' Death warned. 'Eat your breakfast and ride on. Or else you will leave me no choice but to kill you.' Then he looked up at Bates who was standing by the kitchen door, his mouth open with disbelief at what he had just witnessed. 'Fresh coffee. Shawn Hincks is paying.'

'Yes—yes, right—er—right away,' Bates stammered, before running back into his kitchen.

Death picked up the table, but left the broken china that had been his mug and plate where they lay. Almost fastidiously, he put the white cloth back on the table. Then he looked down at the Hinckses. Nathan had got to his knees and was trying to help up his brother.

Nathan turned to glare at death. 'No one treats us this way. No one, you hear me, mister.'

'I hear you,' the man in black acknowledged. 'Just like you to know I just did treat you that way. Don't let there be a next time.'

'There'll be a next time, mister,' Nathan promised, getting to his feet. 'Only we'll be the ones to finish things—permanent.'

'If I may intrude, gentlemen,' Dull joined in. 'I think I ought to warn you that you will be facing Death.'

Nathan Hincks spun around to face the unwanted intruder. 'What you on about?'

'That's his name,' Dull supplied, pointing at the man in black. 'He has killed five men already.'

'Is that meant to scare us?' gasped Shawn, trying to show some bravado despite his obvious pain.

'I thought you might like to know what you're up against,' Dull offered. 'I think he will make you numbers six and seven.'

'The hell he will,' Nathan blurted out. 'He's nothin' compared to us.'

Having said his piece Nathan limped out of the dining-room, the limp more pronounced as he tried to support his winded brother's weight.

Death stared at Dull, who had now resumed eating his cold breakfast. At least he knew where the government man stood from the way he had goaded the two brothers into making the wrong decision. Death knew that the Hincks brothers would be waiting for him the moment he left the dining-room. There was nothing more for him to do except drink the fresh mug of coffee that Bates put before him, after which he would have to face the inevitable.

Slowly he rose from his place and stepped over to Dull, standing at the man's shoulder and leaning over so that his mouth was close to Dull's ear.

'Be careful, Dull,' Death whispered. 'You don't want me to come for you.'

'Make you a deal,' Dull mumbled the offer. 'Promise me that Tunbridge will live.'

'No deals, Dull,' Death's voice grated.

Dull, suddenly, felt very afraid. He did

not want to beg, but he could not help himself.

'If Tunbridge dies,' he pleaded. 'It will be the end of me.'

A faint smile crossed Death's lips as he discovered a weakness in Dull's character.

'Then that'll be the way it is,' Death stated.

Dull looked Death in the face. 'Then damn you to hell, mister. I will do anything I have to to put an end to you.'

'That's your choice,' Death acknow-ledged. 'I wouldn't expect any different from you.'

Dull went to make a retort but it died on his lips. For the man in black was already making his way through the tables heading towards the dining-room doors where, he hoped, two men would be waiting to get their revenge.

Except that Death did not do the expected. Instead, he veered into the kitchen and exited from the hotel by the side door. Then he strolled, unhurriedly, up the alley into the main street.

Shawn Hincks was leaning against the doorway, with a rifle cradled across his waist, which indicated that Nathan was still inside, again with some shelter from which to ambush their target the moment he left the dining-room.

'They say that death comes as a surprise,' Death said, softly, his voice carrying to Shawn Hincks.

With shocked surprise Shawn spun around, the barrel of his rifle coming to bear as Death fired. The bullet struck Hincks in the belly doubling him over. Involuntarily, his finger pulled the trigger to fire a wasted bullet into the boardwalk. He looked up as Death fired again. Shawn Hincks, half bent over, could only watch as his own life ended as the bullet tore away the top of his head. Then he toppled over to dive down the two steps in front of the hotel and crash head first into the dirt of the street.

There was just a few seconds of respite

before Nathan burst out of the hotel, his gun firing blindly at where he believed Death to be. But his intended target had moved further out into the street from where he fired two shots, calmly and smoothly, into the chest of his would-be killer.

The force stopped Nathan dead. He rose up on tiptoe before falling backwards into the hotel. Death holstered his guns, stepped over Shawn's corpse and climbed the steps to the hotel. After giving Nathan a cursory glance, he entered the hotel and went straight to his room.

Dull bowed his head, grimacing at the unexpected end of the Hincks brothers. He had really believed that those two wild boys would put an end to Death and Dull's troubles.

There was nothing for it, he decided, he would have to call a truce with Tunbridge in the hope that they could work together to get rid of this killer.

Angrily, he returned to his room where

he was shocked to find Tunbridge waiting for him. As he entered, Biggelow pushed the door closed and stood against it to prevent Dull from leaving.

'Impressive, isn't he,' Tunbridge mentioned, sitting on the edge of the single bed. 'Your man, is he?'

Dull shook his head. 'Nothing to do with me. Just a bounty hunter.'

'Come on, Willard, you can do better than that,' Tunbridge coaxed. 'That man is executing my men. You are hunting us down, but to keep your hands clean you have brought in your own killer.'

Dull began to pace the narrow room, walking up and down the length of the bed.

'Do you really think that I would stoop that low?' Dull demanded, pausing in his pacing to point an accusing finger at Tunbridge. 'I want you and your men alive.'

'All right,' Tunbridge conceded. 'I believe that you would prefer to take us alive. For what? Will you stand up in court and speak for us? Like hell you will. What happened at Mansfield was as much a fault of yours as it was ours. Also we were at war. Mistakes happen in war. Sometimes, with a bit of forethought, they can be avoided. You claim that Federal prisoners of war were killed at Mansfield by Federal troops. I now know, differently. They were not prisoners, but turncoats who had joined the Confederate Army. These men are innocent of the charges of murder against them. You know that. So why did you suppress that evidence?'

'You cannot prove that,' Dull pointed out. 'If you could you and your men would not be running and hiding from justice.'

'I can and I will,' Tunbridge promised. 'Unless you leave my men alone, call off the gunman now, the file goes to Washington.'

'I tell you, he is nothing to do with me,' Dull protested with an angry flap of his arms.

'But you know who he is,' Tunbridge pressed.

'Calls himself Death,' Dull admitted, slumping down on to the bed.

'As in D-e-a-t-h?' Tunbridge spelled out with a frown.

'Can you think of another way to spell it?' Dull snorted.

'De'Ath,' Tunbridge told him. 'That's how it is pronounced. In Summerhill there's a new marker over Calvin Nicholls' grave. The word De'Ath has been added.' Dull sat bolt upright at this information. 'You recall that the night Nicholls died he received a telegraph to say that his father had died? I think it might be an idea to find out who sent it.'

'We do not have to do that,' Dull stated. 'It all makes sense now. Death sent it.'

'I have to admit, you could be right,' Tunbridge conceded, thoughtfully. 'All we have to do is find him.'

'Room thirteen,' Dull supplied with a

grin. 'I think it is going to be unlucky for him.'

'Let's pay him a visit,' Tunbridge suggested, rising.

'I do not carry arms,' Dull hastened to point out.

'That's not my concern,' Tunbridge retorted. 'You're in this, just as much as we are.' He jerked his head at Biggelow. 'Make sure Mr Dull is not left behind.'

The three men strode down the hall until they reached room thirteen. Dull tried the handle, turning it softly until it swung wide. Biggelow shoved Dull, who fell headlong into the room to lie prone on the floor as Tunbridge and Biggelow levelled their guns, eyes and barrels raking the room searching for a target.

'He's not in here,' Biggelow said, stating the obvious.

'I take it he's not hiding under the bed,' Tunbridge said with sarcasm looking, with disgust, at the prone Dull.

Dull shook his head as he made a

laborious effort to pull himself to his feet.

'Mel,' Biggelow gasped. 'He'll be after Mel Johnson.'

'Dull,' Tunbridge commanded, 'you find him and stop him. Or I will keep my promise.'

Dull was going to protest, but thought better of it. Reluctantly, he left the room and went downstairs. Bates was changing places with the night clerk, Tom Quimby.

'Lookin' fer someone?' Quimby asked, innocently.

'The fellow who called himself Death,' Dull mentioned. 'I wanted a word with him.'

'Too bad,' Quimby said with a shake of his head. 'He's gone. Checked out half an hour back.'

'Dammit,' Dull cursed. 'Where did he go?'

'Didn't say nuthin' to me about goin' any place,' Quimby shrugged.

'Nor me,' Bates hastened to add. 'I'm

just glad he's gone.'

Dull just snorted, turned and walked away. He stood on the boardwalk, looking both left and right, searching for any sign of a tall man dressed in black; a man with a pale face that Dull had half recognized; a face that he should have realized was similar to that of the late Calvin Nicholls.

He also came to the conclusion that he was beginning to make too many mistakes. There was only one way to put matters right and that was to find Mel Johnson and protect him: for where ever Johnson was, Death would not be too far away.

NINE

Tom Quimby was glad to get away from the hotel before any more awkward questions were asked. He had not liked Willard Dull from the moment he first set eyes on him. Even less was his trust for Major Tunbridge whom he regarded as two faced. This jaundiced view came from his knowledge of how much the Major invested in Oakridge while running as a town councillor up in Summerhill. It made a man like Tom Quimby wonder what his game was. Whatever it was, it was not honest and above board.

Quimby, then, did not trust either Dull or Tunbridge even if he could see them. On the other hand the man in black was something else. Death's cold attitude might worry others but it did not make Quimby afraid, for he knew the man, in fact had known him for several years—ever since he had struck up a friendship with the father.

He had been saddened by De'Ath senior's death and had expressed the wish that he had been down for the funeral. Then again, he had to concede no one knew where he was or what had happened to him since the day he had got trampled and crippled by a bunch of steers in the Oakridge stockyards.

He was forty-seven years old, yet he looked younger. He was around the five feet eight mark and weighed one hundred and eighty pounds most of it solid muscle.

If he showed any sign that his injuries had left their mark, then it was not on his face, but in his limp and the slowness with which his left arm would move.

From midnight to nine in the morning he worked as the night clerk at the Bates Hotel, then from half past nine to one in the afternoon he would clean out the stalls at Murchison's livery stables. After a meal he would retire to his sleeping-quarters at the back of the livery, where he would have a good eight hours sleep to awake fresh and ready to go back to work. With his lodgings provided along with two meals, he was able to save most of his wages. Some he put by to secure his future, the rest he had ready to help those who needed help.

In a break from his usual pattern, Quimby headed straight for his quarters. Before he opened the door he took a casual look around to confirm that he was not being watched. Only when he was satisfied did he enter the small room, which was cramped with a single pallet bed, a wardrobe, chest of drawers and a small cooking stove.

Ignoring the man who slept on the bed, he lit up the stove and put on a pot of coffee to boil.

'Hope you've got enough for two,' the sleeper said, removing the wide brimmed, round-crowned black hat that covered his face.

'Whatcha take me fer, Asa,' Tom Quimby grinned, genially, limping over to sit on the edge of the bed.

Death sat up and answered with a rare, but genuine smile.

'Thanks for putting me up, Tom,' he said.

'No trouble, Asa,' Tom grinned. 'What are friends fer, if'n they can't help each other come trouble.'

Death sighed. 'Except this trouble's not your problem.'

Quimby hung his head. 'I'm sorry you won't let me get involved. Calvin was a good man for all his sins. He didn't deserve the death he got. There'll be folks back home who'll think different—him being a man's man an' all that. So he was weak there, but it done nothin' to change the goodness in him.'

'You know, Pa, when he died,' Death mentioned, lost in memory provoked by

Quimby's words, 'his last wish was that Calvin be there for the burying. He hoped my brother would realize that Pa had forgiven him. He made a will and left the business to Calvin.'

Quimby chuckled. 'I thought you'd be Hell's new undertaker.'

'Sure,' Death nodded. 'Got all the skills but I figure the dead should bury the dead, like it says in the Book. I'm a blacksmith and a carpenter who enjoys making things for the living.'

Quimby pursed his lips and glanced at the coffee pot to see if it was bubbling. When he saw that it was not, he turned back to his friend.

'Seems to me you've been doin' a lot of destroyin' of late,' he mentioned. 'Never took you for a killer.'

'Pay back time,' Death said, harsher than he meant. 'They killed my brother. They never knew him—not like I knew him. The people of Hell destroyed him because he was not normal—in their eyes.

Maybe that was why Calvin became a lawman because he knew that he would get killed someday. It would be an end to everything for him.'

Tom Quimby looked up in time to see Death wipe his eyes on the sleeve of his shirt. What, he wondered, would folks think if they saw the human face of Death.

'You knew him better'n me,' Quimby stated, sadly. 'Guess you maybe right at that. Just can't help feelin' that it was a waste of life.'

Death turned and swung his long legs over the edge of the bed and sat upright. The cold mask was settling over his grim features for there were matters of the present and not the past that needed attending to.

'Sorry, Tom,' he said, steel back in his tone. 'Memories I don't need. Not now. Best you get on with your chores and keep your eyes open for Mel Johnson.'

Tom stood up, huffily. 'If that's what

you want. Figured you might like to talk some.'

'Another time, perhaps,' Death said. Then, sensing the hurt he had caused, 'Soon as the coffee's boiled, I'll bring some out to you.'

'Obliged.' Quimby shrugged as he opened the door, ready to get on with his work.

Amos Biggelow was in a belligerent mood by the time he reached Major Tunbridge's suite of rooms at the Cattleman's Hotel. Both he and Mel Johnson had wasted a lot of time looking for the man who called himself Death. Wherever they had gone they had asked the same question only to get a negative reply. It was impossible that such a tall man dressed entirely in black could just walk out of a hotel and completely disappear.

To make matters worse Tunbridge did not believe his report.

'Figure it this way,' Biggelow blurted out. 'Dull fakes that cross to make us believe this fella's Nicholls' kin. He brings in this killer to get rid of us because Dull can't do it any other way. He says this fella's nothin' to do with him—we believe him. He even joins us to kill him, but the Death fella ain't around. Why? 'Cos Dull's already told him to get outa the way.'

Tunbridge sighed as he gave Biggelow a wry look. He was about to tell Biggelow what a fool he was, when he started to rethink what his bodyguard had said.

'You know, Amos,' he said, 'you could have something there. I took everything that Dull said at face value. A marker is easy to put in, to throw a man on to the wrong scent. I know how devious Dull can be.' He stroked his chin, thoughtfully. 'Amos, get back to Summerhill right away. Buy a horse from Murchison and bill it to me. Have a talk to the telegrapher and see if you can find out where that telegraph came from about Nicholls' father and who sent it. I want as much information as you can get me by the time the train gets in.'

Biggelow nodded that he understood his orders. It meant that he would have a lot to do when the Oakridge train pulled into Summerhill. At least he could leave the chore of loading the flatbed wagon to others while he reported in to Tunbridge.

'Sorry to put an extra load on you,' Tunbridge mentioned. 'Especially as you have one task to do, now that Byrd is dead.'

'I can cope,' Biggelow assured him. 'We've had tougher problems to solve in our time.'

'Just one more thing,' Tunbridge added as an afterthought, 'tell that lawyer, Haymes, to mail that parcel.'

'You sure you want that done?' Biggelow asked, surprised.

'Yes,' Tunbridge stated, firmly. 'No matter what happens now, I want Dull destroyed. Maybe, I should have done it years ago—but he and I were friends then. I couldn't betray a friend. Now I know different. He was never anything more than a man who would sacrifice anything and anybody to make sure that no dirt was found on him.'

'Maybe, you're right, sir,' Biggelow acknowledged. 'But I get to thinkin' at times. The way they hounded the James brothers and the Youngers 'cos they were Confederates one time. What have the damn Presidents of this here United States done for us? They got us to fight their damn war, then abandoned us. It's not just us—there's others as well. Ten years on and we're still carryin' the blame for something we was told to do.'

This was a long speech for Amos Biggelow and the first time he had shown any of his inner feelings about events that had affected him.

'At least we are fighting back,' Tunbridge reminded him. 'The future is secure and that file might just do enough damage to let those who are left live a normal life. Perhaps this will be the last train we have to rob; the last army payroll that we have to turn to our advantage. The businesses we all own will keep us until we die of old age.'

'If Death doesn't get us first,' Biggelow growled.

'We will just have to see that he doesn't,' Tunbridge pointed out, then added, more formally, 'Time is wasting. You have things to do and I have to get packed if I'm to make the train.'

Willard Dull, too, was packing his few belongings together, anxious to be ready to make the afternoon train. He was feeling tired and weary after following Biggelow and Mel Johnson around town, asking the same questions and getting the same replies as the others had.

Where was Death?

There was no place that he could hide. There was no one, that he knew of, who knew the man in black. There was only one conclusion to come to and that was that Death had left town. Where? To camp outside the town limits or to Slickett's Hill? The questions that came to Dull's mind were endless. If Death was heading for Slickett's Hill— Then it all clicked in his mind. Death knew about Slickett's Hill because he was a government man like himself. Dull laughed out loud. All the mystery and suppositions that he and Tunbridge had drawn from the evidence that they had was solved. Death was there to put an end to Tunbridge and his men, while he, Dull, was able to keep his own plan running in the dual role of bait—and if the killer did not get them all, then Dull would bring the rest to justice.

No wonder Death would not accept the $5,000 bounty money. The marker in the Summerhill cemetery was a good ruse, changing Nicholls' name to suggest that some kin of his was on a vengeance trial. It enabled both Dull and Death to do the job they had been ordered to carry out without any connection being made between them. The whole theory seemed totally logical to Dull who refused to see any flaws in it—if there were any.

By the time Willard Dull had finished packing his valise, he had persuaded himself into a more cheerful and confident composure.

'You know that's the oddest thing I've seen,' Tom Quimby mentioned, leaning his broom against the jamb of the partly open door.

'What was?' Death asked from within the room, where he watched the comings and goings through the crack that gave him a view of aisle down to the open double doors of the livery.

'You saw Biggelow?' Quimby asked.

'He took a horse,' Death stated tiredly, knowing that Quimby was turning something normal into a drama.

'Bought a horse,' Quimby corrected. 'Charged it to Tunbridge. Now that is odd, because where Tunbridge goes, Biggelow goes. Biggelow's on his way to Summerhill and Tunbridge's still in town.'

Death was silent for a moment as he remembered a fragment of an overheard conversation.

'There's a linesman's shack some place,' Death mentioned. 'You know of it?'

Quimby nodded. 'Sure. About twenty miles from here. There's a steep incline for about three miles. Tell you, by the time it reaches the top you could walk by the train, that's how slow as it's goin'. At the top there is the shack. Deserted though. Hardly been used since the railroad got built. Why?'

'You talk a lot, Tom.' Quimby noticed that there was no hard edge to Death's comment. 'How about telling me where the shack is?'

'Oh, yeah.' Quimby laughed at his own error. 'Between here and Summerhill.'

Death nodded to himself. Perhaps it would be easier for him to ride on and wait at the line shack for things to develop rather than remain cooped up in this room at the back of the livery.

'I think I had better go,' Death said after a few moments of deliberation.

'What about Mel Johnson?' Quimby queried, concerned at the sudden change of plans.

'I'll let him come to me,' Death shrugged. 'I think I know where he'll be going.'

'The line shack,' Quimby guessed. 'Well, I'll get your horse ready for you.'

'Obliged, Tom,' Death said, warmly. 'I'm really grateful to you.'

While Tom Quimby saddled the horse, Death put on his overcoat and hat then sat on the bed to check over his guns before making sure he had enough supplies in his saddle-bags. Satisfied, he stood up by the door waiting for Quimby to signal that all was ready.

Death moved quickly to his horse and mounted up while Quimby stood guard at the door, throwing anxious glances up and down the street before waving Death forward. At a slow walk the horse turned right as it exited from the livery.

Quimby ran with a springing, limping gait until he was alongside.

'Slickett's Hill's that way,' Quimby reminded, urgently.

'If anyone's watching,' Death stated, 'they'll think the same.'

Quimby nodded and grinned as he turned his back on the man who rode down the street to disappear amongst the abattoirs and warehouses.

Ten minutes later, Mel Johnson stepped into the livery to collect four horses, all of which he saddled himself, before mounting a sturdy looking chestnut gelding and leading the other three on a string. He took one look around the stalls.

'Looks like you've been done with business,' Johnson laughed, tossing back his red-haired head.

'We'll survive,' Quimby fired back. 'Gone this long without you.'

Johnson made no comment as he rode to the left of the livery making good time as he took the back trail out of town.

Down the line at Slickett's Hill things were beginning to happen. Two riders came up from the south. Both men were redheads dressed in conventional style western gear. They looked like a couple of cow-hands about to take the train for a good night's fun up at Oakridge.

Another rider came from the east, looking like a drifter. He had long hair and his chin was bristled. Denim pants were tucked into light-brown leather riding boots. He wore a grey shirt that was open to the middle of a deeply matted chest. Dismounting by the trading store attached to the plank station building, he took one look around before going inside.

Deke Tinsley, with Frank and Rufus Johnson had arrived at Slickett's Hill.

The Johnson brothers sat together on a pile of lumber to wait for the train while Tinsley tried to sell his horse so that he could buy a ticket.

Everything looked normal, except that the brown-suited drummer who had accosted Dull the night Lance and Colby had died, knew different. He sat at one of three tables set aside for eating or drinking for those waiting or who had just left the train. A man appearing to mind his own business, yet seeing everything and missing nothing.

Tinsley had to bargain hard before Sid Marsh, the bald, greasy-looking store owner handed over twenty dollars before pulling a warm beer to clinch the deal.

The obese storekeeper ambled out of the store to sit in a reinforced rocker and stare out at the flat featureless landscape. He pulled a big brass watch from deep in the pocket of his apron. One hour seven minutes to train time.

As he put away his watch another rider

came in from the west. Whoever he was, he was in a hurry, the way he jumped from the saddle and dashed into the telegraph office.

'A man in a hurry,' the brown-suited drummer observed.

'Maybe the stage got hit,' Marsh commented. 'Good to see some action around here. Life can get dull at times.'

'Man could die of boredom,' Tinsley spat into the dust, as he brought out his drink.

'Ain't none died yet,' Marsh chuckled, the flab of his belly wobbling. 'Ain't no place to bury 'em.' He kicked the ground with the low heel of his shoe. 'Ground's too hard.'

The drummer smiled, politely.

Tinsley spat. Then took his drink back inside. It was better to be alone than listen to another man's prattle. Walking the length of the store, he took in the stacked shelves, the flour sacks at the end of the narrow room, the counter and the tables opposite. He swung around the counter to look through the curtained door at an untidy, filthy bedroom-cum-kitchen which was empty. He sighed, with relief. At least he was alone in the place and the only way in or out was through the one door. The only windows were those that faced front so that he would be able to see if any strangers approached.

Ever since the others had been killed, he had been nervous. Being hunted was nothing new; he had been chased by posses and bounty hunters before. But one man who seemed to just appear, kill and disappear, that was one man he did not want to meet.

He ambled back to the door and leaned against the jamb.

'Mind if I draw another beer?' he asked.

'Help yourself,' Marsh suggested. 'Just leave change on the counter.'

Tinsley pulled himself another glass of beer after sorting change from the back pocket of his pants. After one look at the head that had frothed up on his beer, Tinsley decided that he would be no good behind a bar.

Once more he ambled outside to lean against the door jamb in time to see Marsh pointing just right of the north. A ragged plume of dust was rising and drifting westward on a light breeze.

'Stage comin' in,' Marsh stated, rubbing his hands together in anticipation that he would get a few more paying customers.

A figure emerged from the ticket-cum-telegraph office, to stare northwards before turning around to cup his hands over his mouth.

'Stage coming up,' he shouted.

'Know that,' Marsh called back, sourly. 'I can see it, Jim.'

The telegrapher and ticket collector, Jim Bowles, waved away the tetchy comment, then glanced around as another man emerged from the office, said something to him before mounting his horse and riding away.

The two men sitting on a pile of lumber on the platform exchanged worried glances. Whatever was going on, they would get to know about it soon enough. For now, it was better for them to keep their minds on the job.

The stage moved closer, its pace slower now as it approached the railroad tracks where boards had been laid to provide a crossing. There were three outriders, all wearing cavalry uniforms. One rode ahead, his bearing suggesting that he was an officer, passing over the crossing about a hundred yards ahead of the coach. He veered away to dismount by the waiting ticket collector. A brief exchange passed between them which resulted in the officer slapping his thigh angrily, while at the same time throwing an anxious glance at the stage which was rumbling over the wooden crossing.

'Wonder what's going on?' the drummer asked. 'Trouble do you think?'

Sid Marsh just shrugged. 'Who knows?

If it's important, Jim'll let us know soon enough.'

'Train's probably running late,' Tinsley contributed, after downing a mouthful of warm beer. 'You get the service you pay for.'

'That's not fair, mister,' Marsh defended. 'Train's never been more'n five minutes late. Known times when it's been ahead of time.'

'Just made a comment,' Tinsley growled, curtly. 'Not lookin' for an argument.'

Marsh and the others watched as the stage was driven to the side of the station. The driver climbed from the box, to start unharnessing the six-horse team and lead them over to a small corral between the station office and store.

'Hi, Frank,' Marsh called out.

The stage driver gave a brief wave as a sign that he was returning the greeting.

The gun guard was still perched on top of the stage his narrow, watchful eyes flicking from the three men standing outside the store, to Frank, to where the officer was seeking information from the station man and hearing nothing that he liked, before gazing at the two red-haired cowboys on the platform. Once in a while he would deviate from this routine to look around at the featureless terrain.

From where Marsh was standing he could see at least three passengers in the coach, none of whom seemed to show any inclination that they were about to disembark.

'What are they waitin' for?' Marsh grumbled, anxious for their custom.

'Shall I go and find out?' the drummer volunteered.

'Free country, mister,' Tinsley stated. 'I know a few people who fought a war to prove it.'

'That right?' Marsh said, interested. 'Thirty-second New York—me.'

'Them's the only two things we have in common,' Tinsley grunted. 'We fought the same war and on the same side. Don't mean a thing, does it?'

'Guess not,' Marsh agreed, sullen now that he would not be able to share anecdotes with a fellow soldier.

Instead, the two silent men watched the drummer stroll over to the stage. To wave a friendly gesture at the gun guard before poking his head through the window.

'Alvin, Curt, Mike,' the drummer greeted, while making signs that suggested to the watchers that he was inviting the passengers over for a drink.

'Ly,' the portly, smooth-shaven and thinning-on-top Alvin acknowledged, before making an introduction to the other two men. 'Lyle Berlin, gentlemen. Our boss, you could say.'

Berlin glanced at a thin, pinch-faced man. 'You must be Mike Russ.'

Russ just nodded.

'Curt Buller,' the other mentioned, like a man who knew that he looked average and was anxious to assert himself.

'Glad to see you.' Berlin's feelings were

genuine. 'Until now you two were just names in a file. I would've preferred to have met you before, but things got fouled up along the line.' He turned to Alvin. 'Everything all right?'

'We've got things under control,' Alvin assured him. 'The payroll will be waiting at Summerhill.' Then he pointed at the four large sacks beside Buller. 'The Treasury Department supplied us with a load of currency they were going to burn. Most of it's worthless but enough is genuine to get a conviction.'

'The act of train robbery is enough,' Berlin pointed out. 'But we need Tunbridge with the money—at least that's Dull's idea. We're here to make sure that we lose nothing.'

'It's just the idea of letting them take it, that rankles,' Mike Russ pointed out.

Berlin dropped his friendly pose. 'You're here to carry out orders. Which is better? Lose a couple of hundred dollars or the whole army payroll?'

'OK. I take the point,' Russ conceded. 'Just don't like people walking over me.'

'Goes with the job, Mike,' Berlin shrugged. 'You'll find yourself doing lots of things you don't like.' He stepped away from the stage to call out, 'If you change your minds, come on over, the drinks are on me.'

As he walked back to the store, he threw out his arms and shrugged a gesture that indicated that he had tried to encourage the passengers to take a drink with him. An illusion, as his mind flicked through the files of Buller and Russ. Both men had been involved in the Civil War as agents, but only Russ had worked with Dull by supplying intelligence from behind enemy lines—and now worked as an agent for the Treasury Department. He had also given evidence at Crandell's trial about the Mansfield massacre: it made him the ideal candidate to be Tunbridge's informant on the movement of Government funds that had been stolen over the years.

That, then, was Lyle Berlin's brief. To find Tunbridge's informant and ensure the safety of the army payroll. Nothing more, and if anything went wrong he had to be sure that one gate was closed and that Tunbridge received no more information.

'Well, I'm going to have a drink,' Berlin announced as he drew level with Marsh and Tinsley.

'Mister, you're goin' to need one,' Tinsley grinned. 'Right after we tell you what we just heard.'

'What?' Willard Dull exploded, a few hours later.

'Told you,' the Oakridge station master said. 'Train's been held up. Won't be here until morning now.'

'But—' Dull blustered. 'I mean how?'

'Let me explain,' the station master replied, like a teacher talking to a five year old. 'Rails are made of steel. They get affected by the heat of the day and the cold of the night. Steel expands with heat. Contracts with cold. Sometimes they get warped out of shape. If that happens and nobody gets to know about it a train could come off the rails. Maybe folks would get killed. Our job is to try and make certain that doesn't happen. Now a crew has gone out to fix the line, but they won't be done until morning. Understand?'

Dull nodded. It was infuriating, but if he was delayed then so was Tunbridge. What difference, he had to concede, did a day make when everything that he had worked for was about to reach a successful conclusion.

As he walked down the platform ready to leave the station and find a room for the night, he spotted Major Tunbridge. He ambled over to him and nodded a greeting when Tunbridge looked up.

'Bad news, Sam,' Dull said, sombrely. 'Train won't be here today. It has been held up.'

Dull kept a straight face as a moment of shock passed over Tunbridge's features. But he laughed at Tunbridge's distress all the way back to the Bates Hotel.

TEN

It was six o'clock in the morning and the main street of Oakridge was alive with people. Many of them were carrying luggage down to the station where the previous day's train was due to arrive within the next thirty minutes.

While others rushed, Willard Dull strolled. To his way of thinking he would still arrive before the train showed a sooty smudge against the lightening eastern horizon. The only thing that he wanted to be sure of was that Major Tunbridge was going to be on the train.

As soon as Dull located Tunbridge, he melted to the back of the crowd and stayed there until the late running train arrived. Satisfied that his quarry was aboard, Dull strode down the length of the line of four carriages and boarded the last of them.

He walked the aisle, squeezing past and apologizing to passengers who were either looking for a seat themselves or trying to load luggage up on to racks. As he moved from carriage to carriage Dull searched for familiar faces. In the third carriage he located the Johnson brothers, both men sitting facing each other in aisle seats leaning forward conversing in low tones.

Dull almost missed Deke Tinsley who was seated just inside the second carriage. His right arm supported his head which was resting against the window as though he was sleeping. Maybe he was, for his hat was pulled down over his face which prevented Dull from seeing Tinsley's eyes.

With a satisfied smile, Dull moved faster up the aisle of the now moving train, to the first carriage where he deliberately sat down opposite Tunbridge.

Tunbridge glanced up. 'Welcome aboard, Willard.'

'To coin a phrase,' Dull smiled, confidently, 'this is the end of the line.'

Tunbridge smiled. 'You really think so? I wasn't going to leave until tomorrow but when I saw you around, I thought—' He paused, as though collecting his thoughts. 'I thought, let's really find out just how good you are. To make all your planning come right, you have to catch me with the others with the money. Just one problem—like the killing of Nicholls, you are going to be my alibi yet again.'

Dull shook his head. 'You do not have enough men, Sam. This time you have to get your hands dirty—one way or another.'

Tunbridge smiled. 'We shall see.'

Mel Johnson licked his lips. He was still half asleep, lying on an old mattress and covered by a worn grey blanket. He had been getting worried when the train had not shown up and it was gone midnight before he decided to bed down for the night in the wooden line shack.

The only furnishings were the torn

mattress dumped in one corner and the pot-bellied stove set in the centre. Two dirt-encrusted windows faced front towards the railroad tracks, while the door was set in the side wall.

This door was now open to let in some light and the stove was alight, flames licking out of the top to curve around a skillet in which bacon and eggs were frying, the smell of which had awakened the recumbent Mel Johnson.

He fisted his eyes as he sat up looking around the empty shack and smiling as he assumed that his brothers had arrived. The relief was replaced by shock as a dark shadow came through the door to check the cooking food.

'Who—are you?' he stammered, searching around for his gunbelt.

'You want breakfast?' the dark voice growled. 'Do you good, you know. Condemned men always get to eat a hearty meal.'

'You killed Lance and Colby,' Mel

Johnson came to conclude, as Death flipped egg and bacon from the skillet on to an enamel plate.

'And Phelan, Byrd and Royce,' the man in black reminded him. 'Not many of you left.'

Death ambled over to where Mel lay and put the plate, with a fork, down on the floor just out of arm's reach.

'Why feed me?' Mel asked with a touch of bravado. 'Waste of food considerin' you're goin'to kill me.'

Death shook his head. 'No reason to kill you. Like always, you get left holding the horses.'

'You touch my brothers, mister,' Mel warned, sitting bolt upright and thrusting out a warning finger to punctuate his words, 'and I'll come after you.'

'Your choice,' Death shrugged, leaning against the door jamb and spooning egg into his mouth directly from the skillet. 'All I'm giving you is the chance to keep your life.'

'Where's my gun?' Mel asked.

'In a safe place,' the man in black shrugged. 'You don't need it.'

'I take it the train didn't go by in the night.' Mel did not turn his comment into a question.

'If it had, I wouldn't have cooked breakfast,' Death stated, tossing the now empty skillet to one side. 'Now if you've finished yours, I'd be obliged if you'd toss the plate and fork over against the wall there.'

Mel Johnson did as he was told.

'Why'd you want me to do that?' he asked, as the plate clattered against the wooden wall. 'Ain't much of a weapon.'

Death moved swiftly and picked up the plate. Then held up the fork.

'That can be dangerous—in the wrong hands,' Death said, a faint smile passing over his lips. 'I didn't figure on getting the point.'

'Ha, Ha,' Mel groaned.

Death ignored him as he half closed the

door, bent down and picked up a coil of rope, which he held up, prominently, so that Mel could see it.

'Time, Mel,' Death said, 'to put you out of action.'

Deke Tinsley kicked out his legs and stretched, before pushing his hat back on his head. He looked around at other passengers, most of whom were dozing, before standing up to leave the carriage. He did not acknowledge either of the Johnson brothers as he passed them on the way to the baggage car.

'Sorry, mister, you cain't go no further.' The voice, which startled Tinsley, came from beside a pile of crates.

'That right?' Tinsley asked, innocently, as the rotund, short conductor rose from a rough wooden chair parked just out of view.

The conductor adopted an apologetic look. ''Fraid not, mister. Cain't have folks wanderin' all over the train.'

233

Tinsley smiled. 'Guess not.'

He turned, appearing to go back the way he came, then swivelled around holding his gun by the barrel. The conductor collapsed quietly as the butt cracked against his temple, as the elder of the Johnson brothers stepped inside, moving swiftly forward to catch the conductor and lower him to the floor.

Neither man said a thing as they moved through the baggage car to stare out at the caboose. Johnson jumped from the platform to that of the caboose, where he flattened himself against the wall. Gently, he edged his way closer to the window set in the door and peered through. Three men were grouped around a plank set across a couple of crates, busy playing cards. None of them were facing the door.

Johnson circled his finger and thumb together, then jerked his head to indicate that it was safe to cross over. Tinsley nodded, before glancing over his shoulder to be sure that the other Johnson was covering their backs in the baggage car.

With a quick bound, Tinsley crossed over to the caboose. He reached down to grip the door handle, then threw an apprehensive look at Johnson before plunging downwards with his hand and shouldering the door open. Both men spread out, their guns covering the three startled, seated men.

'Do nothing silly,' Tinsley warned, thrusting his gun out at arm's length 'Some things are worth dyin' for—but not this.'

'Nobody is going to do anything,' Alvin murmured, more intent on studying his cards than the two gunmen. 'Just take the money and run.'

Tinsley stared at the speaker. Something was wrong; he could feel it. Then he jumped as a shot rang out and the seemingly unworried Alvin slumped forward on to the table, tilting it upwards, revealing his killer's gun as it arced towards the other agent and fired another killing shot.

'Leave the money,' Curt Buller suggested. 'It's a plant. If any of it's genuine, then it's going to be just a couple of hundred.'

'Who the hell are you?' Tinsley demanded, keeping the casual killer covered.

'Curt Buller,' the killer told him. 'My cousin Emily had a brother-in-law Brad Jarvis. Does that help?'

'The name I know,' Tinsley acknowledged. 'Him an' me used to be good friends. So—'

'So you go and tell the major,' Buller cut him short. 'The payroll is already at Summerhill, waiting to be loaded on this train.'

'What do we do now?' Johnson asked, confused.

'Throw this lot over the side,' Buller suggested. 'It's useless. Oh, and put a couple of bullets into me, before you go. Won't look good if I come away unscathed.'

Tinsley glanced over his shoulder. 'Best let Tunbridge know what's goin' on.'

Johnson nodded and left Tinsley alone with Buller.

'You know, mister, somethin' ain't right,' Tinsley mentioned. 'This is all too—too—'

'Casual?' Buller supplied, nonchalantly.

'Yeah,' Tinsley nodded. 'I mean you sit there all calm and gun down them two fellas, then tell me you're workin' with the major. Only none of us knows about you. Figure you to be too clever for your own good. Bye-bye.'

Tinsley fired twice into Buller's chest. Then watched as the man slumped over with a soft sigh of sadness.

'Sorry, fella,' Tinsley shrugged, as he holstered his gun and turned to pick up the four money sacks that the dead men had been guarding. 'Sometimes you have to go with the instincts—right or wrong.'

Tinsley closed the door behind him, then tossed the money bags over to the younger

Johnson who scooped them up and loaded them into two open crates. Nobody said a word as both men nailed shut the crates addressed to Amos Biggelow at Summerhill. All the while Tinsley was troubled by what Curt Buller had said and began to wish that Abel MacGrath was still around to tell him what to do. It figured that Tunbridge had to get his information about the payrolls from somewhere—but somehow Buller did not seem like an informer. Maybe it was just his casual manner—Tinsley put the thoughts aside. It was nearly time to leave the train.

The elder Johnson returned with a grim face that looked as though it was going to spit fire.

'That friggin' Dull's with the major,' he grumbled through his beard. 'So cain't tell 'im nuthin'.'

'Never you mind,' Tinsley decided. 'When we get off, we ride across country to Summerhill. If that fella was tellin' the truth, then we'll take the money from there.'

'Bet ya it'll be well, friggin', guarded,' Johnson snarled.

'Doubt it,' Tinsley responded, lightly. 'No one's expectin' us.'

Death stood in the doorway of the line shack and stared down the grade waiting for the moment when the train came around the long climbing curve. In the time he had been waiting he had made a small change to the building which would give him a slight edge. He had removed some of the planks from the back of the shack which would, if necessary, give him a bolt hole.

Mel Johnson tried to struggle against the ropes that bound him, but he was tied up by a man who knew his business.

'Mister,' he called out, causing Death to glance back over his shoulder. 'How much longer?'

'If I was the engineer I could tell you,'

Death replied. 'You'll just have to wait, just like me.'

'My hands are numb,' Mel grumbled. 'Can't feel a thing.'

'Be grateful,' the man in black mentioned.

'For what?' Mel sulked.

'You're still alive,' Death reminded him. 'I could've killed you hours back—but I don't kill without a reason.'

'But you've got one to go after my kin with,' Mel snapped back.

Death nodded.

'What reason?' Mel demanded. 'At least let me know why you're gunnin' for them and not me.'

'Calvin Nicholls was my brother,' Death stated, tonelessly.

'Oh, hell,' Mel muttered, shaking his head.

'You could say that,' Death agreed. 'That's where they're heading.'

The conversation was brought to an abrupt halt as the sound of the train whistle reached their ears. Death stepped outside to look down the track to where black smoke was thinning as it was blown over the edge of the cutting. Within seconds the slowing train came around the curve, steam shrouding the cattle-catcher and curling around the tank as greater pressure was exerted to propel the train up the steep grade.

'Don't you want to gag me?' Mel asked. 'I could warn them.'

Death shrugged. 'Do whatever you want. Makes no matter to me whether you shout out or not. Those destined to die—will die.'

Tinsley and the Johnson brothers stood poised on the platform of the baggage car, preferring to jump from in front of the caboose as their escape stood less chance of being observed. From their vantage point, they could see the shack and cursed the slowness of the train that kept it so far away. It seemed to take an age before they were able to jump on to the dusty, rocky ground, rolling over a couple of times before any of the trio were able to gain their feet.

'Mel,' called out the elder Johnson dusting down his pants as he peered around for his absent younger brother.

'In here,' Mel called back out of reflex, which he immediately regretted; then tried to shout a warning, which was curtailed as his brother charged through the open door.

Death's gun spat lead twice and Johnson crashed backwards through the door his hands scrabbling at the two fatal chest wounds.

Tinsley watched, stunned, as Johnson rolled over on to his stomach to lie still. Then he drew his gun as he ran to flatten himself against the wall. He angled along it until he reached the open doorway as the other Johnson stepped through the door, throwing himself forward, eyes and gun raking the seemingly empty room. It took too long for his eyes to adjust to the semi-darkness, but they still widened when they saw the figure rise up from behind the pot-bellied stove. The bullet that killed Mel Johnson's surviving brother took him straight between the eyes.

Tinsley was tempted to call out in an attempt to discover who had survived.

'If you're out there, Deke,' Mel yelled out. 'You're on your own. All my kin're dead.'

There was no mistaking the sobs in the youngster's voice and Deke Tinsley felt his own sense of loss. Only a matter of days ago there had been eleven of them, now there was just four. They had to be avenged, but first he had to find the killer.

Instead, the killer found him. Death stepped around the back of the shack and stared at Deke for a moment.

'It's time to say goodbye,' Death intoned.

Tinsley spun around, straight into a snap shot that took him in the chest, left of centre. A neat killing shot. Death walked by the trio of corpses and stepped back into the shack, where he reloaded his gun.

'All done, mister?' Mel asked, his eyes now red from weeping for his dead brothers.

'Just one to go,' Death stated.

'Then me,' Mel stated. 'They might've killed your kin, but you done for mine. I'm goin' to have to come lookin' for you.'

'Like I said, before,' Death told him, 'your choice.'

Death moved away to find his horse and took up the lead of another for he was going to have to ride fast if he was to get to Summerhill ahead of the train.

Amos Biggelow did not let his relief show when he got the news that the train had left Oakridge. Instead he busied himself with hitching up the team to the buckboard, ready to be driven down to the station. Then he collected and loaded a sawn-down, double-barrelled shot-gun which he shoved underneath the seat. Biggelow did not expect trouble, just preferred to be ready if it came.

After checking a brass fob-watch for the umpteenth time, he hauled himself up on to the driver's box and clucked the horse into forward movement. It was still fifteen minutes to train time, but once in a while, when the train was running late it could arrive a touch earlier if the engineer was able to make up time. A rare occurrence, but it happened that way.

He drove by the station to a point two-thirds of the way down the platform, roughly where the baggage car would come to a halt. With a mixture of encouragement and curses, he coaxed the team around until the tail of the buckboard was up against the platform, a manoeuvre completed just as a stagecoach pulled up close by, from which stepped an army sergeant and three troopers who took up position around it.

Biggelow wondered what was going on,

then dismissed the matter from his mind for there were more important things to attend to, and there were more distractions, in the shape of other wagons parking alongside ready to take their shipments that were coming in. It was beginning to get a bit crowded and Biggelow was thankful that he had decided to get in early.

Into this congestion stepped Death.

'Biggelow,' he called.

The big, bald-headed man turned around, his expression unchanged as he looked down at the man in black. He sat there, his big square hands resting on his knees. With unexpected speed he launched himself off the seat, four hundred pounds of solid muscle and bone that slammed into Death, sending him crashing to the ground, where he lay sprawled while Biggelow climbed to his feet, gun in hand. Death rolled to one side, his left hand snatching the gun from its holster. He triggered two rapid shots into Biggelow's chest. The big man reeled back from the impact, coming up short as he collided with the wagon wheel. Breathing heavy, he let the revolver fall as he groped beneath the seat for his shot-gun, which he swung around aiming at the still prone man in black. Death fired, carefully, before Biggelow could shoot. The first shot tore the big man's throat away, while the second passed through his right eye. Dead on his feet, Biggelow pulled the double trigger that released a widening cone of shot that tore a hole in the stagecoach.

The whole scene was shrouded in thick smoke and steam as the train pulled into the station.

ELEVEN

Death knelt at his brother's graveside and looked across at Pam Ross.

'It's over,' he said. 'Rest in peace, Brother.'

Pam stood up and looked down at the man in black. 'When you're ready, I'll cook dinner for you.'

'Obliged,' Death acknowledged.

Pam offered a weak, friendly smile. 'I suppose you would prefer to be alone right now.'

'If you wouldn't mind,' Death smiled back. 'Later, I guess, I'll have to tell you about him.'

'If you think you have to.' Pam tried to make a dismissive gesture with her hand. 'Only if you think it's important.'

'Calvin would think so,' Death told her.

Pam just nodded her understanding, before walking away to leave Death alone with his grief.

Tunbridge and Dull disembarked from the train and were drawn into the recent drama. Both men went over and joined the crowd that had gathered to view Biggelow's corpse and the damage to the stagecoach, from which two troopers were dragging a strong box.

'Wonder what that is?' Dull thought out loud.

'Maybe we'll never know, Willard,' Tunbridge answered, more concerned about the death of Biggelow.

Dull followed Tunbridge's gaze. 'Looks like he got them all.'

Tunbridge shook his head. 'Tinsley and the Johnsons will have survived. Your killer would have to know the plan to have got to them.'

'True,' Dull had to agree.

'It would appear that neither of our plans have worked,' Tunbridge commented.

'Not yet,' Dull grimaced. 'We will see what happens when the others come in to town.'

'You might have a long wait,' Tunbridge pointed out. 'How about a free night or two at my hotel?'

'Why not?' Dull consented. 'Shall we go?'

They walked up the street, two men who had liked each other in the past; enemies in the present who were silent now, until they came to the graveyard, where Dull stopped.

'I want to look at that marker,' Dull explained. 'I just want to be sure that what you told me was true.'

Tunbridge raised an eyebrow. 'You think I lied to you?'

'You should know me,' Dull mentioned passing through the gates of the graveyard. 'I always like to double check things.'

'Like you did over the Mansfield massacre?' Tunbridge snorted.

Dull did not answer. He was watching

the black shadow of Death as it seemed to rise up out of a grave.

'Death,' Tunbridge breathed.

'That is he,' Dull confirmed.

The man in black turned around slowly until he was facing both men.

'You're going to die,' Tunbridge snarled.

'Has to happen sometime,' the man in black shrugged.

'Tell me,' Dull interrupted, 'are you finished?'

Death nodded. 'Biggelow was the last.'

'You forgot about Tinsley,' Tunbridge responded, confidently. 'There are still three—'

'You'll find him and two of the Johnson brothers down by the railroad track,' Death confirmed.

'Dead?' Tunbridge asked, shaking his head with disbelief. 'You've wiped out my entire command.'

In his anger, Tunbridge snapped back his jacket and went for the gun in a shoulder rig. His hand had hardly curled around the butt when Death drew and fired.

'Don't,' Dull screeched, holding out his right hand at Death as though trying to ward off the killing shots, while at the same time attempting to shoulder Tunbridge to one side.

He failed in both attempts as Tunbridge died, and the second bullet meant for him shattered Dull's left shoulder instead. Dull spun around, his arms flailing, as he collapsed on top of Tunbridge's corpse.

'You have killed me,' Dull groaned, clutching at his shoulder.

'Just wounded,' Death observed as he tugged Tunbridge's gun from his grip and thrust it into his own belt; then explained, 'Removing temptation.'

'Finish me,' Dull commanded. 'You have as good as killed me. Tunbridge had a file—it will destroy me.'

'That's the way it has to be then,' Death shrugged. 'Nothing to do with me.'

'Wrong,' Dull attacked, scathingly. 'Everything I planned—'

'You want to know something?' Death demanded. 'When a man makes plans, he thinks he's in control. Thing is he never has control and when things go wrong, he still tries to make the plan come out right. The only thing you can be certain of—in life anyway—is just one thing. You know what that is?'

'Go on,' Dull prompted. 'Tell me.'

A faint smile flickered over the man in black's lips before he said, 'Death.'

This Large Print Book for the Partially sighted, who cannot read normal print, is published under the auspices of

THE ULVERSCROFT FOUNDATION